I0718301

LEGACY

PRAISE FOR THE GIFTEDVERSE

This one kept me interested from the very beginning. With a lot of drama, intrigue and some magic, it's fast paced and entertaining.

— DOODLE BUG

…This trilogy is action packed from start to finish with love and loss along the way… From first book to last, the Owens women will keep you fascinated.

— SUNNI

Packed with excitement, danger, adventure and a roller-coaster ride of emotions. I couldn't put it down until I finished it!..

— CYNDEE MARLING

Wow. That is all I can say about this book. It kept me on my toes waiting to find out what came next. It was well-written with a lot of character and world building.

— SARAH COLEMAN

THE GIFTEDVERSE SERIES

In reading Order:

<u>The Owens Chronicles</u>

Prophecy

Destiny

Legacy

<u>The Gifted Chronicles</u>

First Life

Second Chance

Third Eye

<u>Companion Volumes</u>

Annabelle

Etta

Find out more at

www.giftedverse.com

LEGACY

THE OWENS CHRONICLES
BOOK THREE

AMANDA LYNN PETRIN

CHAPTER ONE

Tears blurred my vision, but I didn't want to see the scene playing out around me. Embry was a dozen feet away from me, face down on the wet, muddy ground. I couldn't tell where he got hurt, but the overwhelming amount of his blood mixing into the puddle beneath him told me I lost him. Gabriel was fighting with everything he had, gaining the advantage as he returned the attacks blow for blow, even though there were four of them and only one of him. I knew he was exhausted, but he wouldn't show it until I was somewhere safe. Or he died.

A hatred like I had never known overcame me as I rushed to attack the man in front of me. He had introduced himself as Henry, but as far as I was concerned, he was the devil incarnate. I had the dagger in my hand, but my arm froze in midair, barely an inch from his chest.

"I admire your tenacity, but there really is no need for all of this bloodshed." His tone was conversational, which made my blood boil. He had stood back and watched his men fight, waiting for me to be exposed. Embry's death was the opportunity he was waiting for, but I was not in the mood for conversation.

"You could have fought us yourself instead of sending your slaves." I struggled with all my strength, but my arm wouldn't budge. My strength should have included magical powers, but the lack of them, and the gown

I was wearing, reminded me I was Cassie. She had been reluctant to fight at first, because she knew Henry's Gift was controlling other Gifted, making them do despicable things against their will. It wasn't until the choice was killing strangers or watching Embry die that she jumped in. Not that it made a difference.

"There would be no need for any of it if you just came willingly."

"So you can kill me?"

Henry was staying alive to complete a ritual that would allow him to take over the world. That would be enough to resist him, but as the Bearer of the Crescent Moon, my heart was the crucial ingredient in his ritual, and I much preferred my heart inside my chest. I shot up my knee, aimed at Henry's crotch area, but like my arm, it froze before reaching its target. Instead of keeping it there, he slowly lowered it back to the ground, with my arm following suit, landing at my side. It felt like a bucket of ice water poured over me as everything tingled for a second, then went numb.

"Death is only temporary, Cassandra. And as you are the blood of my blood, I would never allow any harm to befall you."

"Is that part of your ritual? Blood of my blood?" she spat at him, but I just felt sick inside.

"Once upon a time, Annabelle was my wife. Margaret was my daughter. The last thing I want is for anything to happen to you. Or Corinne." The way he said Cassie's daughter's name, I couldn't tell if it was a threat or a promise. Either way, it sent a shiver down my spine.

"You're attacking us. Hunting us." Cassie shook her head, struggling to figure out if she believed him. Having seen how this scene eventually plays out, I wanted more than anything to show her my thoughts and memories. To warn her.

"Only because they won't let me get close to you." He blamed my guys. I turned to see where Embry was still lying on the ground, but I couldn't see Gabriel. My heart stopped as I searched through the bodies in the mud, but Henry was halfway through saying Cassie's name before he collapsed onto the ground at my feet.

"Are you hurt?" Gabriel asked, as the feeling returned to my body. I

nodded, looking down to Henry, who was unconscious. He wasn't dead, but even his death wouldn't have been permanent. As a Gifted, he would keep coming back until he got what he wanted. Me.

I WOKE up in the passenger's seat with a jolt. *It was just a dream,* I reminded myself, holding on to the door of the old station wagon while I waited for my heart to slowly regain its usual rhythm. I was used to these dreams from my ancestors, and much preferred the ones that happened when I was already sleeping, but these memories felt just as real as my own.

"Tennessee," Gabriel told me before I could ask. He ran his hand through his mess of black hair, though I think it was more about the uncertainty we were facing than the hours spent in cars. Over twenty-four hours since we left New Orleans, and we were only two states over, which would make sense if we were stopping to check out the sights and enjoying sit-down meals, but we barely stopped long enough to go pee and change drivers. With this kind of non-stop driving, we should be home already. Instead, we took forever so the army of Gifted loyal to Henry couldn't find us; bouncing around Points C to Z. If someone was following us, they would attack us out of sheer annoyance from all the detours, without waiting for reinforcements. Unless their Gift was saint-like patience.

Since Gabriel was at the wheel, it meant Embry was sprawled out across the back seat, napping until we stopped for gas or to change cars at some hole-in-the-wall. The guys took turns driving so we wouldn't have to spend the night in any sketchy motels and risk what happened last time. I wasn't up to losing any more people, so I didn't argue.

"Do you want me to drive for a bit?" I offered, but I knew the answer would be no. Gabriel enjoyed having a plan and being in control, so our current lack of a concrete plan was making him hold tight to anything he had control over. Not that I blamed him.

We were going up against the man that they stay alive to protect me from, and our only plan was to get more magic. Hopefully from the books locked away in my bunker. It was less than encouraging.

"I don't mind driving," he assured me. "Keeps me alert." His hair was sticking up a bit in the back now, which made him look younger than he usually did. More vulnerable somehow.

"How much longer until we get to the plantation?" I switched positions to get comfy, but there wasn't much I could do after this long in cars. I knew how far we were distance-wise, but they could easily extend it into next week.

"We could be there by tomorrow evening," he said with a shrug.

"You want it to take longer?" I asked.

"No, I'm good with the pace and eager to get you somewhere easier to secure." He checked his mirrors, all three of them, more to make sure no one was following us than for road safety. "But we have no control over Henry's followers. If there's a car that exits when we do, or takes the same turns, we have to lose them before moving on."

"We could also stop so you guys can rest. Maybe eat some food that doesn't consist of microwaved grease?" I suggested.

"That may be pushing it." He smiled at me, more like an equal than when the summer began and I was an intolerable teenager he had to keep his distance from, "But if we find a safe enough location, maybe."

"I was kidding. Constant driving is great," I tried to sound convincing, but he still turned to look at me, not buying it. So far, every 'safe' place we went to ended with someone getting hurt. Usually, it was a Gifted who would come back to life, as long as their life's purpose wasn't accomplished yet, but not always.

"Should I be like Embry and remind you how hard this journey would have been in a carriage pulled by old horses, with the blistering sun beating down…" He did an excellent job of pointing out how much worse this could be. Embry and Gabriel would both fit in with me and my friends if I ever made it to college, even if they were closer in age to the founders of Harvard than its current students.

"I'll check the sarcasm." I sighed. I was grateful he made a joke about it instead of the annoyed silence he would have given me at the beginning of the summer.

"Don't worry, I can handle it," he assured me, smiling to himself as he checked his blind spot. I looked out the passenger-side window so he couldn't see me blushing. We had a long road ahead of us, and my feelings for Gabriel were the least of my worries.

CHAPTER TWO

The sun was setting as we crossed through Virginia into Maryland, a mix of purple, red, orange, and pink. It was beautiful, but Embry had used the sunset as his i-spy the last three rounds. We were entertaining ourselves in the back seat while Gabriel was at the wheel, again.

"I'm sure there are rules against using the same thing each time," I complained after it took me over twenty-one guesses to ask if he was spying the sunset again.

"I think it makes it easier for you," he argued. "And that's how you played."

"I used a different tree every time," I argued, remembering how annoyed Sam would get with me. My surrogate big brother would play along and was nice about it, but even as a child I could see him rolling his eyes. Sam got his payback when it was my turn to entertain his daughter, Clara. Embry was the only one I believed was having as much fun as I was, even after playing for hours. I should have known then that he was just a master at hiding things.

"*That* should have been against the rules." Embry shook his head as we came up to a slowdown in traffic. It was long past rush hour, but there was smoke up ahead. I craned my neck to see what was going on and saw a car go up in flames. The sirens were blaring from somewhere behind me, and I knew they were coming closer, but the sound was getting lower and lower, until I couldn't hear it at all…

I was Beth, as she and Embry got ready to go to the theatre, reminding me so much of Sam and Deanna. They touched each other every time they passed by; hand grazes, running her fingers along his back, wrapping his arms around her and snuggling into her neck to get something in front of her instead of just reaching for it... They were young, happy, and in love. Which was saying something with Helen and Jack constantly demanding their attention. I couldn't help but smile every time Jackson had a story to tell me in his toddler babble, and I could feel Beth's heart melt when Helen asked if Daddy wouldn't mind being the one to braid her hair.

Once everyone was ready, the four of us took a car into town. It appalled me that their version of a car seat was letting the kids roam around the back seat, with Beth putting her arm out if ever there was a sudden stop. Thankfully, Embry drove the smoothest drive I have ever been on, considering the unpaved roads we took. He parked on the street, and we walked to the theatre. Jackson fell asleep in the car, so I carried him in my arms, something I haven't done since Clara. Beth and Embry were in step, holding hands and looking up to smile at each other continuously, while Helen skipped along a few feet in front of us.

"Helen wants to bring you to show and tell tomorrow," I said when we rounded the corner, letting go of Embry's hand long enough to get the theater tickets. It was September 5th, 1926.

"For my magician act? Does she want me to sing?" Embry teased, but Beth was serious.

"They're supposed to talk about their hero," she explained.

Embry processed the information, then asked, "What about you, or... wasn't she going to talk about David?"

"David was a kind man, and he would have been an incredible

father... but he died. You're the one who is raising her, the one she looks up to. She wants to be like you."

"Nothing would make me happier," he said before leaning over to give his wife a kiss.

Once we entered the theatre, Beth insisted that we sit in the front, so they could be close to the action. Embry laughed at her, but agreed, and got two seats in the front row. Jackson chose his father's lap, but Helen sat in her mother's.

It was halfway through the play that it started. It was hot in the theater, but not stifling, so I had no reason to think this was anything other than a happy memory, until I smelled smoke. Beth stood up and looked towards the doors, where there was smoke coming from the lighting room. As the flames became visible, everyone rushed for the exit.

Embry was ahead of me with Jackson, while I held on to Helen, my hands on her shoulders as the crowd pushed into us. She was holding onto Embry's coat as I tried to protect her from the people rushing for the door, but somewhere in the shuffle, someone let go.

"Beth!" Embry called when he realized I wasn't following. I could hear him yell, again and again, getting farther and farther away as the crowd pushed against us, so many people making a wall between Beth and everything she cared about.

"Get the children out. Save them," Beth called.

"I'm not leaving you," Embry argued, having to yell really loud for me to barely hear him.

"Get them out. Then you can come back for me, but they're what matters," she yelled, as they pushed him towards the exit and I lost sight of him. We tried to get to the doors too, but someone pushed me, and I fell. Everyone behind me kept coming, none of them looking down. I tried so many times, but I couldn't get up. Every time I did, all I saw were flames, before someone knocked me back down to the floor. It looked like hundreds of people blocking the exits, so even if Beth kept going, she wouldn't make it out. I clutched the ring Embry gave Beth, then closed my eyes and let the flames come. Just like Annabelle had...

. . .

"WHAT DID YOU SEE?" Embry asked with concern, bringing his hand to my arm when I screamed. I didn't mean to push it off, but I still felt like I was burning, choking on the smoke.

"I am so sorry." I could feel the tears pouring down my face and my skin was in agony, but it was my heart that broke for his. "Why didn't she use her magic?" I had tried, knowing I had no control over what happened in the past, but I couldn't understand why Beth didn't. She was a favorite of mine, especially after staying in her house and finding out her secrets. We both had magical powers in common, and she seemed like she had so little fear and was always up for a challenge. Centuries after Annabelle died, I still wear my hair the same way as all my ancestors, except Beth, who defied cultural norms and cut it like a boy. I saw her in my mind as a brave trailblazer, not someone who sits back and lets awful things happen to her.

It took Embry a moment to understand what I was talking about, but I saw his face drop, the pain written in every line once he did.

"I don't know," he said, pulling me as close as he could with my seatbelt. Gabriel was quiet in the front seat, but his eyes were locked on my reflection in the rearview mirror, full of concern.

It was my second time dying as one of the Bearers of the Crescent Moon, but I'd also seen Rosie the night she passed. I always knew it wasn't me, that I was just having memories from women who looked exactly like me, but they felt so real to all the senses. Cassie and Beth were obviously a few years older than me, but not that many. Probably around Sam's age.

I never thought much about it, because they always looked to be roughly the same age in all the memories, but this was the third death and none of them looked older than thirty. If I assumed Annabelle died not long after returning to Boston with Margaret, we were four for four on Bearers dying young.

I remembered Annabelle's tombstone from the cemetery at the plantation. I did the math of 1692 minus 1664, which told me she died around twenty-eight. I couldn't remember the exact dates for the others, except for Beth dying in 1926, but I knew where to find them.

"What's wrong?" Embry asked when I reached for the backpack at my feet.

"I need to check out something in the Chronicles," I dismissed him. I could find out a lot quicker if I asked them, but looking it up in the written account of my ancestors' lives would let me prepare for answers I was pretty sure I didn't want to know. Embry went back to his seat behind Gabriel, but kept an eye on me.

Annabelle's entry in the Chronicles confirmed the dates I used. Rosalind's death in 1778 also put her at twenty-eight. Which could be a rather weird coincidence… only Cassandra lived from 1822 to 1850. I wasn't surprised, but my heart rate – that had finally gone back to normal – was becoming erratic again.

I shut the book but kept it in my lap, holding on to it so my hands wouldn't shake. It felt like I was suffocating again, only this time it wasn't from smoke. I could see both the guys staring at me from the corner of my eyes, but I wasn't ready to confront them yet. There had to be an explanation.

I bit my bottom lip to push away the anger and tears so I could think. It was looking like each of the previous Crescent Moon Bearers died before reaching their twenty-ninth birthdays. In distinct ways. Some predictable, but others not. Henry had a hand in both Annabelle's and Cassie's deaths, but I don't think he would intentionally give Rosie tuberculosis without taking her heart, especially when she was so weak. And setting an entire theater on fire was definitely overkill to get to one person, considering how many of them escaped. Still, they couldn't all be coincidences.

"When was Beth born?" I asked Embry, trying to sound like it was simple curiosity.

"May sixteenth," he answered without hesitation, but gave me an odd look. We both knew I wasn't into horoscopes, and it wasn't like I would need to wish her a happy birthday on the day.

"The year?" I pressed, trying to look on the bright side. The odds were that I would survive another nine years, but all I could focus on was the fact that I would die. If I was right, even if we defeated Henry and somehow made it through, it would only be temporary. Sam's sacrifice would be for nothing.

"1898." Embry furrowed his brow while attempting to figure out what I was getting at, but I felt like someone had grabbed my heart and was crushing it. Beth was twenty-eight.

"Is there anything you would like to tell me about all the Crescent Moon Bearers?" I asked, focusing on Gabriel.

"What?" he sounded confused.

"Is there something about Annabelle, Rosalind, Cassandra, and Elizabeth that one of you should have told me by now?" I rephrased my question, turning to Embry. He used to be the one to tell me things, once upon a time. My eyes were glistening, but I refused to blink and let the tears fall.

"We have centuries of knowledge on your family, Lucy, we obviously can't have told you everything." Embry was getting worried, but neither of them seemed to know what I was getting at.

"How old was Annabelle when she died?" I asked Gabriel.

"Twenty-eight," he said like it still stung.

"And how old was Beth?" A shiver went through me from the memory, still so fresh in my mind, and my skin. I skipped the others and stuck to the two that affected them the most.

"Twenty-eight." I could see Embry's brain working, doing the same math for Cassie and Rosie. "But that's…" he tried to reason it away.

"It's not a coincidence that Beth was trampled, suffocated, and burnt alive at the same age as Annabelle," I argued. "Cassie and Rosie were also twenty-eight." I handed him the Chronicles.

"We knew they died young, but… No one gave Rosie tuberculosis. Annabelle chose to sacrifice herself for Margaret. And no one could have predicted the lighting room would catch fire. It's just a coincidence," Embry tried to convince himself.

"I thought the Universe sent you guys to protect me, not that I would die either way." I shook my head and stared out the window.

"No, there is no curse on you, no other prophecy, nothing that implies the same will happen to you," Gabriel argued like he wouldn't accept the alternative.

"Except for precedence and the lack of a single exception." I wanted to throw up. "Stop the car," I said evenly, clenching my jaw to stop the tears.

"Luce," Embry tried to talk me down.

"I need some air," I pleaded. "Whether or not you accept it, there's a distinct possibility, that even if Henry never gets to me, some force out there will make sure I never make it to thirty, and right now I can't breathe." I aggressively rolled down the window. "You guys help me survive and make it through all the attempts to kill me, but maybe you're just here so they can't complete the ritual. Because that's the endgame. You help me survive as long as I can, then make sure Henry doesn't get my body when it happens?" I felt sick.

"That's not how it is," Embry argued.

"Neither of us is resigned to you dying. And if his plan wasn't to kill you, I would rather you be with Henry than be dead," Gabriel said, the vein in his forehead pulsing as he tried to control his emotions and the car.

I would call him on his lie by telling him I knew they would kill me themselves rather than let Henry do what he had to with me, but when his eyes met mine… I believed him.

"Whether you like it or not, I will die when I'm twenty-eight, won't I?" I stopped being angry and turned vulnerable, which felt worse.

"It's a possibility," Embry said after considering it.

"That we will do absolutely everything in our power to make sure doesn't happen," Gabriel assured me.

"Please stop the car." The numbness in my voice scared me, which is probably why Gabriel pulled onto the shoulder. The child lock was still on the doors, so I looked over to him. His eyes were pleading with me not to go, but he pushed the button to let me out. I shut the door and walked towards the wooded area beside the highway.

I looked back to see them looking after me before I kept going, past the tree line, into the dense parts where the remaining bits of sun struggled to get in. It was only once I could no longer hear the cars that I truly let the implications hit me. No matter what anyone did, within ten years, I would be dead. I brought my hand up to run my fingers through my hair, an attempt at self-soothing, but ended up pressing my hand to my forehead as a searing pain shot through my skull.

CHAPTER THREE

It was like Mr. Fraser, only a million times worse. Instead of the pressure of a hand trying to get into my brain, this was like a hot iron of electricity burning its way in. Even if I tried to stop it, there was nothing I could do.

"You've discovered the curse." Henry's British accent filled the surrounding forest, as it felt like all the heat and light disappeared, leaving nothing but darkness.

"Where are you?" I asked, turning around in circles. My head was in agony, but I couldn't let him kill me without a fight.

"You're cute, pretending you don't know what I'm talking about." I could hear the smile in his voice, but couldn't see him anywhere, "You only have to hold out ten more years to make sure I can't complete the ritual."

"How do you know?"

"Donovan may have been your target, but someone should have told you the dangers of soul magic," he warned. "It was brave, but terribly foolish."

"There's a fine line between foolishness and bravery," I shot his own words back at him. At the time I found it endearing, how nervous he was to ask Annabelle out. It was before I knew he was a Gifted who's purpose was to rip her heart out.

"Touché." There was sadness in his tone, but how would he know about the memory dreams? "You don't have to die like the others."

"I won't come willingly," I argued.

"I'm not offering to spare you, Lucy. I still need your heart, but I have a spell, taken from a grimoire, that can save you." It sounded too good to be true, which meant it probably was.

"You're trying to kill me, remember?"

"I am. But a long time ago, the one I was trying to kill was my wife." He almost sounded sorry. "I had to resign myself to doing that, but I never stopped looking for an alternative. Eventually, I found a solution."

"Congratulations." I turned around again to make sure that he and his minions wouldn't jump out at me.

"At the moment, it's more of a success for you than it is for me. I have hidden somewhere very safe, a spell that restores you back to your life as you left it. A complement to the ritual that would have saved me centuries had I found them at the same time."

"What do you mean by restore me?" I was curious in spite of myself.

"There is a spell that will bring back one of those marked by the crescent moon. Unlike your companions and myself, who come back exactly as we were the first time we died, without aging, this spell would fully restore you, as if you never died at all. You could live a full life, get married, have children, and forget all this nasty business ever happened."

"That's impossible," I argued, but all I could remember was Annabelle's certainty that she would be back. What if this was it? What if she knew there was a spell, and she thought the guys would use it to bring her back?

"I assure you it isn't."

"Show it to me," I asked with a confidence I didn't feel.

"Join me and the spell is yours. No more limits on your life, no one chasing you… you would be free."

"I don't trust you." I wanted to run away to show him I didn't want anything he had to offer, but since he was in my head, he would most likely follow.

"You don't have to trust me, because you already know I'm telling you the truth, and as honorable as it might sometimes seem, you do not want to die," he said with an edge that filled me with anger. True as it may be, his price wasn't something I could live with, even if it gave me a happily ever after. "You know where to find me if you change your mind," he said before the pain in my head disappeared, and I knew he was gone.

"ARE YOU OKAY? WHAT HAPPENED?" Embry was the first to reach me in the woods. He put his hands on my arms and checked me for wounds as Gabriel came over.

"He's gone," he said, having probably run around looking for Henry.

"We heard your scream, but by the time we got to you there was some kind of barrier, and we couldn't get in," Embry shared.

"The essence tracking I did to find Donovan was soul magic. He wasn't really here," was my way of explaining that I gave him a way into my head. I could remember the chill I felt when it seemed like Henry saw me through the tracking. Turns out I wasn't being paranoid.

"What did he want?" Gabriel stayed close to me, but his head turned at every sound, analyzing it to see if the maker was a friend or a foe. It was nearly pitch black now, so far from street-lights, with the trees blocking the stars.

"He tried to get me to go with him again."

"After they killed Sam?"

"He knows that we all die at twenty-eight," I admitted.

"It could be a coincidence," they both argued.

"But it's not," I told them, apologetic even though it was my life we were talking about. They wanted so badly to believe that it wasn't true. That the other Bearers' deaths were nothing more than a series of unfortunate events at the same point in their lives.

"How do you know? Did he explain it?" Gabriel asked.

"Not really." I waited until they both looked up at me expectantly. "He said he could save me."

"By bringing you back with magic after cutting out your heart." I could see Gabriel's anger and lack of trust for Henry.

"No, he said it was a spell from a grimoire. One so I won't die when I'm twenty-eight. If I give him my heart, he'll give me the spell that brings me back like nothing ever happened. I can grow old and have kids... the whole nine yards."

"A spell?" Gabriel was skeptical.

"I know we obviously can't trust him, but I also don't think he's lying. There's always a cost with this kind of magic, and it'll probably be one we are not willing to pay, but it can't hurt to look into it, right?"

"Why would he even have something like that?" Embry asked.

"He said that once upon a time, the heart he needed was his wife's, so he tried to find a way to keep her alive," I said like it was a ridiculous idea, but part of me believed him.

"That alone would make me not trust him," Gabriel pointed out. I nodded, not wanting to show how badly I wanted to. "But if there's even a possibility of a cure, then we'll find it," he decided. "We save you and destroy Henry." It was optimistic and overly ambitious, which was weird coming from Gabriel, but he was so sure of himself that he nearly convinced me.

They started talking about logistics, and different people they could ask about the cure, but my mind was on the spell, and its potential price.

"Ready to go, Tesoro?" Embry asked when he saw they'd lost me.

"I'm sorry, I wasn't paying attention," I apologized. "I was just thinking that if the spell needs me to cut someone's heart out, I would rather die. Unless it was Henry's. Maybe."

"You don't have to worry about that," Gabriel said without meeting my eyes, as if my shoes were interesting enough to capture his attention.

"Even if I'm not the one who has to cut it out," I amended.

"We don't know what it entails. Life and death spells are a big deal, but since your death would result from a curse, maybe it won't be that heavy. If it's some horrific spell that requires baby sacrifices, then we'll find another way. But if it's a line the two of us are prepared to cross, then you don't have to worry about it," Embry assured me.

"And you two never heard anything about this?" I verified.

"No, but we haven't been asking around and searching for it either," Gabriel reminded me.

"What if Annabelle knew?" I ventured. "What if when she told you she would be back, she meant that spell? Henry said he took it from a grimoire. What if it was hers?"

"I am sure she would have told us if she had a spell she expected us to recite to bring her back to life. Otherwise, we failed her miserably," Embry pointed out.

Gabriel looked to Embry and sighed, probably thinking, like me, that my ancestors kept a lot of things from them. "Have you figured out a way to zoom in on a single memory, to get them at will? Or are you still getting them whenever they want to come to you, like when you're sitting in a tree or about to jump off a balcony?" he asked, his hands bound tightly into fists at the memory.

"I don't control it, but there are triggers. My first Henry memory happened after I saw his picture in a book, being in her bedroom let me see Beth, sometimes I get memories from other people when I'm touching them... It could be coincidence, but I think I can influence it," I shared.

"I don't think we have anything of Annabelle's." Gabriel turned to Embry.

"I might have had something at the villa, but most of her stuff is back at the plantation," Embry agreed.

"No jewelry, a family heirloom... nothing?" I pressed, but Embry shook his head for each one.

"We don't really have much of hers either way. Clothes don't keep for centuries, she was wearing the jewelry that really mattered to her... apart from the Chronicles, it's mostly just a few things back in Boston..." Embry was dissuading me, but Gabriel was hiding something.

"What did you think of?" I asked him, not even waiting for Embry to finish.

He looked to me like he wanted to deny it, but I initiated a stare down that he eventually had to turn away from. "The dagger you used on Donovan at the motel... it belonged to Annabelle's father," Gabriel admitted.

"But..." There had to be a reason he was so reluctant to share.

"It was her father's, not hers, and they've been passing it down for generations. Not to mention you stabbed Donovan with it, so his blood was the last thing it came into contact with."

"That ship has sailed," I assured him with an involuntary shudder. "Let's do this," I said with as much conviction as I could muster.

CHAPTER FOUR

We had to find a safer place than in the middle of the woods with the car parked on the side of the highway, so Embry drove us to a college campus and sweet-talked the librarian into letting us use one of the quiet study rooms.

I knew the chances were slim that it would work, since I really didn't have a handle on the memories. At all. I still didn't know if they were to help me or to kill me. Or if Annabelle even knew anything for me to find. I based this theory entirely on her habit of keeping things from people, so it wasn't a lot to go on.

I took the sapphire-encrusted dagger in my hands and thought as hard as I could about Annabelle, and a spell to bring her back.

I could feel the guys watching me, waiting to see if it would work. I was about to give up and tell them it had been a ridiculous idea of mine, when the room faded away…

"Are you sure you know how to use that?" The Gabriel standing in front of me was maybe twelve years old, and though he was questioning Annabelle's skills, he was looking at her like she was God's gift to mankind and could do absolutely no wrong.

"Of course, I do. My father taught me how to take care of myself." Annabelle was holding the dagger in her hand, but I could sense her fear, both that her father would find her in his study, and that the sharp blade would cut her.

"I'm sorry I doubted you." Gabriel smiled and looked at her in a way that made her heart beat faster, but she knew it was forbidden.

"Look..." She pulled away before the moment could go too far, twirling the dagger like she had seen the men by the docks do whenever they wanted to impress the ladies.

Twirling was going better than she expected, but she got overly confident and threw it up in the air. She caught it in her left hand without a problem, but when she tried to throw it back to her right hand, it spun too much, so she caught the blade instead of the handle. It sliced into her right palm, which as long as I was in the memory, was also mine.

"Ow!" she muttered under her breath. They would be discovered if she cried out any louder, but boy did it sting.

"Are you alright? I'll go get your mother," Gabriel offered, taking a step towards the door.

"No, you can't!" Annabelle bit her bottom lip and let out a sharp breath.

Gabriel looked at her, considering it, then sighed. "The bandages are still in the cupboard?"

"Top shelf," she agreed.

"I'll be right back." He shook his head at her before quietly exiting the room.

Once Gabriel left, Annabelle dropped the act and cradled her injured hand to a chorus of "Ow, ow, ow, ow, ow!" until she heard him coming.

"You should sit down and keep it above your heart," Gabriel suggested, helping her to her father's chair.

She bit her bottom lip the whole time he wrapped the white bandage around her palm, holding her hand in his as he did. She took deep breaths against the pain, but also because he was so close and touching her in a way he'd never done before.

"There. All better." Gabriel kissed her hand before looking up at her, *and in the moment that his lips were on her soft, damaged skin, the pain went away. Or at least she didn't notice it over the excessive beating of her heart...*

"It didn't work?" Embry and Gabriel were by my side when I came back.

"Not the right memory," I argued, trying to ignore the spark I felt when Gabriel touched my hand. I told myself it was the remnants of the memory and tried to push the thought away.

"There has to be something..."

"What about the empty pages?" Embry perked up.

"What?" Gabriel asked.

"The blank pages Beth left in the Chronicles?" It took me a minute to clue in, but Beth left a bunch of empty pages right in the middle of her section in the Chronicles. Not to mention random drawings from her daughter, which were cute, but not what I was hoping for when reading about her outstanding adventures.

"I'm just thinking out of the box."

"It's worth a try, but I don't know how I could reveal something she hid in there..." I grabbed the Chronicles and rifled through the pages as I spoke, eventually stumbling on one of the blank ones, before I got a flash of Beth transcribing something from a frayed piece of parchment.

"Was that another one?" Gabriel asked. It wasn't a full memory, so I didn't pass out, but he was right by my side.

"Just a flash. I don't know who originally wrote it, but Beth copied it in here."

"It could be invisible ink," Embry suggested, but even he didn't think it was likely.

"I doubt this is a 'lemon juice to a candle' type of operation," I argued.

"Guess you'll have to intend it into revealing itself," Gabriel tried to make me laugh, earning a tiny smile.

I closed my eyes with my hands on the page, visualizing the flash of Beth writing it down.

"That's amazing," Gabriel prompted me to open my eyes as ink formed its way into words across the page, like an invisible hand was writing it.

"It's magic," Embry teased, but I was too busy scanning the page to make sure I didn't have to kill anyone.

"Kiara's Cure," I read the title.

CHAPTER FIVE

"The herbs and powders will be easy to find, but I don't know where we'll get some of the other things on this list," Embry said once the invisible hand finished writing out ingredients that had to be combined under the light of a waxing crescent moon. "We can manage something from each of the Crescent Moon Bearers who came before you, but stuff from your mother and father… I don't even know who he was."

"I thought you were friends with my mother?" I looked from one to the other.

"I checked in on her, but your Grams only wrote to me after you were born, and he was already out of the picture by then," Gabriel explained.

"I know he broke her heart, but she didn't want to talk about it," Embry added.

"Charlie knew," I admitted, pulling the envelope from my backpack. "My grandmother kept in touch and wrote letters to him."

"I'll go find us a car while you read it," Gabriel decided after a student looked in to see if our room was occupied.

"We'll meet you out front," Embry said, nodding for me to open the envelope.

INSIDE WAS a collection of letters between Charlie and Grams. I read them while we slowly walked to the front of the building. The first one was sent a couple of years before I was born.

"It's just Grams explaining to him that my mom wouldn't be visiting him that summer as planned."

"When is it from?" He came closer to put a hand on my shoulder.

"Two years before I was born." I checked the date again to confirm.

"She needed to stay home and get more chemo," he said like it still hurt.

"She got cancer *after* I was born," I argued, even though it was there, blue on white, in Grams' handwriting.

"Who told you that?" He seemed genuinely confused. "Your mom was dealing with leukemia since she was a kid. She was the bravest little girl I ever met, fighting it with everything she had, beating it, then starting all over again when it came back."

"I guess I assumed it was new; that she wouldn't have a kid if she knew she was dying," I explained. It was weird, thinking of her as her own person. It was easier if I pretended she was someone I didn't really know or care about, but at the same time, I didn't. She was my mother, and I loved the idea of her, of what she would have been for me. Her death left a terrible void in my life and in my heart, but I didn't know her at all.

"I think we were all surprised, but it also made sense. I went to see her in the hospital when she was maybe twelve, and she told me the one thing that really sucked about dying young was that she wouldn't get to be a mother."

"The one thing?" I raised an eyebrow at him.

"She got good at resigning herself to the other things," he defended her statement.

"This one mentions a boyfriend," I said of the next letter. "It sounds like Charlie knew him. Grams is worried because no matter what, someone's heart gets broken."

"Does he have a name?"

"Brian. No last name." I handed him the letter.

"Brian Sherwood?" he suggested, scanning the page.

"Who is Brian Sherwood?"

"He moved in with his grandparents on the other side of the swamp when he was eleven. He worked for me a few summers, trying to get money to cover his grandmother's hospital bills. When Charlie and I found out what he needed the money for, we covered her expenses, and he kept working as a thank you. One day he said he didn't need our help anymore, and I don't think I saw him again," Embry shared.

"Why would you think of him? Is it just for the name or do you think he could be my father?"

"I know he met your mother when she came to stay the summer. He's in some pictures from the album I gave you," he remembered. "They got along, but she had to leave mid-July because they accepted her into a drug trial."

"Did it work?" I asked of the trial, getting a nod. "Was he nice? A good guy?" I wanted him to say yes. "But I guess if he was nice, he wouldn't be my dad, because no good guy would abandon his pregnant girlfriend, then not even visit his daughter once after her mother dies of cancer." I crossed my arms and huffed. I wasn't sure what I was hoping to find out, because the outcome would be the same. Good guy or bad, he wasn't here.

Embry looked at me like he was surprised I had this pent-up anger at my father. I didn't seem like I had daddy issues. The truth was, I had so many other issues to worry about that my heartless father wasn't usually worth mentioning.

I grabbed the next letter, but only had time to make out the first tear-smudged line in my mom's handwriting, asking if Brian's family still lived nearby, before I was back at the manor...

"Can I see her?"

A guy, roughly my age, was standing in front of me, holding my blanket. It wasn't monogrammed, so I couldn't be positive, but it had the pink heart in the corner. There was so much pain and regret on his face, but every fiber of my being, of my mother's body, was tense. She was on high alert in case he tried to get past her to the bassinet in the corner, and to make sure she stayed strong instead of falling back into his arms. Looking at how torn up he was, I did not understand how he could have left her.

"No. If I have my way, you will never see her. Ever. So when she asks about you, I can pretend it didn't work out and you left without knowing about her instead of having to tell her the truth; that you never wanted her. That you asked me to get rid of her."

"Will you let me explain?" he pleaded like it was the one thing in the world he had to do.

"I don't want your lies and trying to get me to forgive you."

"You will hate me a lot more than you'll want to forgive me," he admitted.

"Then why bother?" I could hear her thinking that she didn't know if she could handle another heartbreak from him.

"Because you need to know," he said with an intensity that had her nodding even though she didn't really want another reason to hate him. "My mom had this friend, a guy who would come by and see me every once in a while, even after she died. When you went back home that summer, he came to me and offered to bring me to Boston with him. He said I could work for him and pointed out that I needed to get out of the house, away from death and watching her suffer and... I couldn't do it anymore," he said, knowing she wouldn't be happy with him because she was dealing with cancer just like his grandmother had.

"I never asked you to come."

"He did." I could feel that her heart was breaking more than ever with those two tiny words.

"He did?" she repeated, hoping she had it wrong, or that he was referring to his heart in the third person. Anything other than what he was confessing to.

"My mom's friend. When I went to work for him, he told me it wasn't necessarily a real job, but that you really enjoyed your summer, and as long as I hung out with you, he would cover my tuition and an apartment down here for school."

"He paid you to spend time with me? Who the hell was he?" She let the anger take over so she wouldn't start crying.

"I didn't know who he was, but at first, I thought it was sweet that he wanted to take care of you like that."

"You liked the money, and it was pathetic, not sweet." I could tell that she didn't believe the first part, no matter how much he hurt her, but he was looking at her like it got worse.

"It was neither. It was selfish and despicable and horrible," he admitted. She was about to ask what he meant, but he launched into a confession. "When I found out why, I wanted to stop. To leave, but I was in it too far by then. Not just because of the money I owed him, or the threats he started making, but I cared about you, and I knew that if it wasn't me, he would find someone else."

"I'm a human being, Brian, I don't just like people because some guy wants me to. And why would he care who I hang out with?"

"He didn't. He wanted you to fall in love with me." He looked disgusted with himself, but had to say it anyway.

"Why?" she asked.

He explained, starting with Annabelle, about the copies, about one of her descendants being crucial for some ritual, how Henry hunted them through time and didn't have what he wanted yet.

"I don't get why he sent you. Did he want me to trust you so you could kidnap me and take me hostage?" I could tell my mom was only pretending that this was all news to her. Grams must have shared bits and pieces with her about the two guys who stopped by sometimes.

"No, he wanted me to make sure you would continue the line." And there it was. The guilt was plain on his face, but he didn't look away from her. He looked us straight in the eye and took what was reflected at him, knowing he deserved it.

"He sent you to sleep with me?" Her voice broke. She was horrified, and I didn't blame her. I felt dirty, betrayed, and disgusted, not just because she was, but because my father just admitted that someone paid him to impregnate my mother...

I was sitting on a bench outside the library when I came back to the present.

"What did you see?" Gabriel was kneeling in front of me.

"My mother," I admitted.

"And?" Embry was sitting beside me on the bench, his arm around my shoulders, probably to hold me up when I passed out, but I wiggled away from him. I didn't want anyone touching me right now.

"The blanket I packed... it was my father's." I only told them what they needed to know.

"That's it?" Embry pressed.

"The blanket was his," I repeated, then handed him the letter to put in my backpack, that he was now carrying, before I walked past them to the parking lot.

"Lucy..." they called after me.

"I don't want to talk about it." I turned and put my hands out, grateful I didn't accidentally blast people anymore.

They looked at me, then at each other. They must have decided the conversation could wait until later, because they shrugged and followed me out.

Gabriel got us a black SUV, so I tried to go into the back row where I could be alone.

"I'm exhausted, if you wouldn't mind navigating," Embry asked me, a clear ploy to prevent my solitude, but I was too drained to argue.

I sighed and took the passenger's seat. I could feel both of their eyes on me, even as Gabriel watched the road and Embry pretended to sleep, but I couldn't face them right now. My insides were in knots and all I felt was shame. It wasn't just the Henry parts; all of me was rotten.

CHAPTER SIX

I stared out the window even though I couldn't see past the headlights. My father's confession was heavy on my mind, and my heart. I'd thought it was bad that Henry was Margaret's father, but it hurt a lot more when it wasn't just a distant ancestor, but the man who fathered me. At Henry's urging.

"Am I still heading for the plantation?" Gabriel asked, interrupting my thoughts. Embry never would have let the silence last that long, but Gabriel understood keeping it all inside.

"Isn't that where the books are?" I asked without looking at him.

"It is," he agreed. "But if we're tracking down things that meant stuff to your ancestors, the best place for Cassie..." He let the thought linger, waiting for me to catch on.

"I can't."

"Can't, or won't?" he asked. "And why?"

"Because I can't face them. Until I see them, they get to live in a world where they're worried about us, but they still think Sam and I will come home to them. Once we go to the Beach House, I won't be able to lie to them, so I'll have to tell them Sam is dead because of me. They'll never be happy again, they'll hate me, and I will lose what's left of my family," I said simply, though it was anything but.

"First, you will always have me and Embry." He waited for me to look at him before going on. "And second, the girls aren't there anymore."

"What happened? Where are they?" My heart raced, pounding against my chest.

"It's October," he said like that explained it.

"What does that mean?"

"Clara had to go back to school. They're staying with Deanna's dad and being careful. With increased protection," he told my horrified look.

"You're letting Clara go to school?" It was reckless. What if Henry made good on Donovan's threat and went after them to get to me?

"Clara isn't the one they want, and I told you she is being watched."

"I guess you never promised to protect her." My blood was boiling. I wanted to call Deanna and warn her to run and hide and never let Clara out of her sight, but I didn't have a phone, and had no idea where I could send them to be safe.

"You're upset, so I will let that one slide, but we would never do anything to put Clara or Deanna in danger. There are people who have put their lives on hold to guard them, 24/7, and make sure nothing happens to them."

"I'm sorry," I mumbled.

"I know. And I know it's hard, not knowing how to keep them safe, but you have to trust that we're doing everything we can."

"Of course."

"So, the Beach House…" he tried after a few minutes of silence.

"If they're not there, we might as well. That's where most of Cassie's stuff ended up, right?" I didn't know how real these women were when I would go to the Beach House every summer, but there was a room above the garage that held wooden chests, crates, and luggage from way before even Grams was born. I only went inside once, but their age. and the bright yellow color of it all suggested it might be hers.

"After Cassie died, Corinne couldn't stand the Beach House or any of her mother's gadgets, so she left them behind and moved back to the manor."

"She didn't miss her?" I asked, thinking of how often I had bribed Sam to bring me to my mother's room so I could play with her things and feel like I was close to her again. "I mean her things."

"She did. After a few years she came back to the Beach House, eventually brought her daughter and told her all about Cass... but to her, the Beach House was where she waited in fear to find out her mother died, filled with the things that got her killed."

"At least the manor had a lot of happy memories for me."

"The family summered at the Beach House, so I imagine she had a lot of those too, but in the winter Cassie and her band of saviors used it as their base of operations to fight crime. I don't think Corinne knew anything about her mother's vigilante activities until she was locked in the house with nothing else to do but explore. Alan defended Cass, but he didn't want Corinne to know that they might hunt her too, so he let her think her mother died for getting involved in other people's problems."

"It was her lair?" I focused on my ancestor's activities rather than her daughter's pain. She never mentioned a Batcave in the Chronicles.

"It was less of a secret lair and more of a place of business." He made it sound less cool, but when you were in the business of defending the helpless, your coolness was a given.

"Did they have a sign on the door with their team name?"

"It was more of a word-of-mouth operation, but they got stuff done."

"I read," I agreed.

"That book was a fraction of what she and her friends accomplished. If she thought it was paranormal or was likely to happen again, she put it in the book, but they accompanied women home late at night, rescued children from abusive homes, housed the poor and desolate…"

"Cassie was a saint," I summed it up.

"She was… sometimes."

"Sometimes?" I raised an eyebrow at him.

"Don't get me wrong, she was amazing, with a heart of gold, but she would never turn the other cheek, or a blind eye to suffering. She ruffled more than just a few feathers in her day."

"And still managed to be the perfect eighteenth century woman."

"Only because she had money and a rich, influential husband who loved her unconditionally, just the way she was."

"Sounds like a badass role model to me." I sighed and turned to look out the window. I hated being that teenager, who is all sighs and woe-is-me, but this wasn't about silly high school things.

"That she was." He smiled nostalgically. "What's on your mind?"

"Maybe we're wasting our time." I shrugged.

"Maybe," he agreed. "We don't know how powerful Henry is, or if anything will work, but I could never forgive myself if we didn't try."

"But maybe we shouldn't," I pressed.

"Are you afraid?"

"What if I'm not supposed to live because I'm not a good person?"

"That's ridiculous."

"Not in a silly way. In the 'we created a man whose mission in life is to kill you and we believe so strongly in this that we will make sure he can't die until he accomplishes it' way."

"He told you his mission is to complete the ritual, not to kill you," Gabriel argued.

"The ritual involves ripping my heart out. That doesn't sound good."

"Just because it's his mission doesn't mean it's right. You've seen it yourself. Some Gifted are downright evil. That's why there's debate on the name, because a lot of us consider it a curse, and we can't reconcile God giving these Gifts for evil people to use in terrible ways."

"You're proving my point," I told him, but I also made a mental note to ask him about his beliefs some other time. I never thought of him as religious, but they said his mother was devout.

"Some of us are evil, Luce. There's a balance. Sometimes terrible things happen to ensure better ones will come. Some missions get misinterpreted, some never come true. Maybe Henry is here to complete his ritual, but Embry and I are here to protect you and make sure that doesn't happen. Two to one sounds to me like the odds are in your favor."

"Maybe you're just supposed to protect me so I can continue the line, or so I die at the right time."

"I don't believe that."

"Maybe I was supposed to be stronger, and I failed."

"You didn't fail anything. Nothing that happened was your fault."

"I know that in the big scheme of things, you're right. I didn't ask for any of it to happen, and I was an innocent bystander when it started. Only I wasn't. I am the descendent of the man who married Annabelle for her birthmark, so he could kill her. Who hunted his daughter, and generations of granddaughters, ever since. All so he could be powerful. A man who not only does terrible things, but makes innocent people do terrible things to other innocent people, when there's nothing they can do to stop it."

"I never pegged you as someone who so deeply valued nature over nurture," Gabriel said, as if it disappointed him.

"Sometimes nature wins." I stood my ground.

"How can you say that when you are nothing but kindness, warmth, and generosity?" He asked. "It isn't our DNA that defines who we are, it's our choices. The things we do time and time again, day in and day out."

"You're trying so hard to protect me, but maybe I shouldn't be saved."

I turned to look out the window and pretended I couldn't feel him looking at me with even more concern than before.

CHAPTER SEVEN

I used to love coming to the Beach House in the summers. There's an old photograph of me on the beach with my mom, where she's bundled up in blankets with a mustard print scarf on her head, but my most vivid memories are of building sandcastles with Sam when I was little, then with Clara once I got older.

We parked in the garage at the bottom of the hill and made our way up the wooden boardwalk, with Gabriel in the lead. When I was little, it felt like a secret entrance to a magical land, because you couldn't even see the house through the tall grass until you got a few minutes into the path.

It was a long walk to the house, even with the boardwalk Grams put in for my mom's wheelchair. I can't imagine how they did it before, walking fifteen minutes through the sand and jagged rocks. Sam told me they used to come by the water if they had lots of bags, or if mom wasn't in the best shape. There was a dock right outside the house that only we could use.

The Beach House didn't have a key hidden under a flowerpot, but it usually had a lockbox under the porch swing, to the same effect.

"It's not here," I let them know after extensively feeling

around. I even got on my hands and knees to look better, but there was no box.

"It doesn't take a key anymore." Gabriel pointed to a little grey box, like the ones from the plantation.

"Of course, technology." I sighed before putting my thumb on the screen. "Ow!" I brought my finger to my mouth and sucked where the needle had poked it.

"Your fingerprint, DNA, and heartbeat match," Gabriel read off the screen.

"That's way more secure than the plantation," I pointed out.

"The Beach House was remodeled later." Gabriel shrugged before putting his finger on the screen and stepping inside once the house cleared him.

He said they remodeled it, but everything on the inside looked the same as it had last summer. It was a mixture of seaside escape and old-time sophistication, which made sense now that I knew more about Cassie.

"We can stay the night and get back on the road in the morning," Embry suggested, walking around with Gabriel to make sure we were alone.

"I'll check out the garage." I headed for the door.

"Wait, we'll come with you." Gabriel followed me. I was about to argue and remind them I could manage it on my own, but he had a look of determination, not concern. This was more about me choosing an object that represented Cassie than about my safety.

To get to the garage, which held our boat, you could either walk outside or go through the basement that had a tunnel to connect the two structures. Which was apparently the safest place in case of an earthquake. Sam and I would explore it, pretending it was a cave because of all the treasure trunks at the end.

This time, the guys went first, with less adventurous exploration, more making sure none of Henry's men were camped out waiting for us.

It was no longer a pressing concern once we saw the entire path was covered in a thick layer of dust. If I had to guess, I would say it hadn't been used since the summer I was six. Sam and I found a rat in the tunnels and decided to never go back.

There was a door at the end to get to the garage, but it hadn't been updated with the exterior, so all you needed to get in was a key.

"Did anyone grab the key from the hook?" Considering Henry had been after us since before Cassie bought the Beach House, it was ridiculous that we used to protect ourselves with a lock box under a swing and all the other keys on a rabbit foot keychain in the kitchen.

"I'll be right back," Gabriel disappeared, which left me alone with Embry.

AT FIRST, we both stood in silence, waiting for him. I still didn't feel like talking, but Embry kept opening his mouth like he wanted to say something.

"Can you feel feelings too?" I asked, realizing I should have figured this out ages ago.

"I can't read thoughts, but I can sense moods," he admitted. "Although I don't need powers to read you. The amazing little girl I met at a funeral, whose heart is bigger than anyone I know, who has gone through so many hardships, but still smiles at strangers..."

"I haven't been that girl for a while," I argued, wondering if I ever was. "What's that?" I changed the subject, focusing on the burgundy bag he had in his hand instead of on my pity party.

"This is your piece of Beth." He looked at it a moment before handing it over, as if it really was a piece of the woman he loved.

The pouch had a clear jewelry bag inside, with a velvet box I recognized immediately. "Are you sure?" I handled it like it was made of the most delicate porcelain. I opened the box and saw the slightly charred ring Beth was holding when she died. It was damaged beyond repair, but I completely understood all the preservation measures he used on it.

"The more it meant to her, the stronger the spell will be," he said simply.

"Thank you."

"I don't know what you saw about your father, but you're not evil or broken Lucy."

"I know," I assured him.

"Got it." Gabriel rounded the corner and showed us the rabbit foot keychain.

They had me wait on the stairs while they went to make sure the garage was safe.

"It's clear." Gabriel came back for me after a few minutes.

I followed him into the garage. It surprised me that the boat was as big as I remembered, even if I was significantly taller. 'Beloved Lyn' was etched on the side of it, named by my grandfather for his wife and daughter, Evelyn and Marilyn. Grams never sold it after he died, or even when my mom did. I guess the Boyds had been waiting for me to grow up to do something with it, but there wasn't much point to it now.

I went upstairs to the room of chests and old luggage. The colors were faded, but the smells of salty air, moth balls and adventure had me smiling. I took it all in and knew I could spend days going through it all and still have more to see.

"Is it stronger if she wore it often, or loved it lots?" I asked when the guys joined me. Part of the discoloration was from the cobwebs that covered nearly every inch of the room, so I grabbed the wooden handle of an old mop and got to work.

"Emotional attachment. Unless it's something like a brush that has her hair on it; some piece of her," Embry shared.

"Bonus points if it fits in a Ziploc bag and doesn't weigh twenty pounds."

The old suitcases weren't locked, but they were closed tight and hard to open, so I let the guys do the honors. The first one held clothes, perfectly pressed and folded as if she were going on a trip with them. Beautiful and bright colors in the softest fabrics... but not what we were looking for. The second chest we opened had piles of books on history, geography, etiquette, and politics. In the middle of the two piles of textbook-like volumes was a well-read copy of Mary Shelley's Frankenstein.

"Was she a fan of horror?"

"Not so much as when the second edition credited a woman as the author." Gabriel shook his head with fondness for my ancestor before opening another suitcase full of pamphlets and essays attempting to give women equal rights.

"She was extraordinary."

"They all were," Embry agreed, but you couldn't quite compare the richness of Cassie's life to any of the others.

"Cass just got a lot more done," Gabriel understood.

I DISCOVERED a little more about my ancestor with every box. The most interesting one was filled with gifts from Alan. I couldn't tell you what half of it was, but nothing was as it seemed. Shoes had spikes or knives that sprung out, purses had secret compartments, necklaces held pepper, and bracelets acted as rape whistles. Every piece I picked up was more interesting than the one before.

"Driving gloves?" I asked of a pair of creamy white gloves at the bottom of the chest, preserved in their own box.

"Cass was more of a walker," Embry argued.

"Try them on," Gabriel suggested with a knowing smile.

"They're very stiff." It wasn't like she never used them... they were quite worn in that respect, but it was as if there was a spine to them.

"Now put them on again while pushing into the top of them…" Both Embry and I looked at Gabriel like he lost his mind, before I did as I was told.

"What the—" Blades came out of the fingertips like claws, and there were gems on the knuckles to put more oomph in punches.

"That's why she was so upset when I brought the black ones…"

"And there should be padding at the knuckles for when she uses the ornamental birth stones…"

I could hear the guys were still talking, but I was drifting off to a memory, alone in a dark alley. There was a chill in the air that made me shiver, but Cassie ignored it and wiggled her now clawed fingers from inside the driving gloves. She focused on every sound, and I could tell that she wasn't afraid to be walking alone at night. She was hunting something. There was a dripping sound coming from a nearby roof and she followed it instead of running away or waiting for backup.

"Hello?" she called once we reached a dead end. If ever I had any doubts about Cassie's courage, it disappeared as I felt how calm her heart was as she stood in the alley with no escape, hunting an unknown monster without magic or reinforcements.

The wind answered her call, carrying drunken laughter from somewhere close by, and the faintest whimper of a woman who sounded like she was close to giving up.

Cassie took off at a run, taking turns faster than I saw them coming, before we rounded a corner and found a man standing over a woman. I couldn't make out much in the darkness until the moon shifted and revealed bright red blood staining her blue dress.

The man froze when he heard Cassie running towards him, clumsily swinging a cane to protect himself. Cassie stopped the blow from reaching her and used her hand like a cat uses its paw, managing to scratch his face. He roared out in anger, and we struggled over the cane before Cassie used her knee to get him in the groin. Cassie had hoped the woman would get up and run away while she fended off the man who assaulted her, but her injuries were much worse than expected, and there was no way she was getting away without a lot of help. The man was winded for a second or two before he charged at Cassie, pushing us into the brick wall to our right. Cassie reacted before my mind recovered from the push, shoving him off and grabbing his arm with her gloved fingers, causing him to cry out in pain. He looked at her face, which I imagined was terrifying to behold, because all I could feel from her was determination and anger, not a drop of fear. He seemed to consider it before running off down the alley.

We ran after him, but the woman whimpered again, and there was no way she would last the night if left to bleed out on the sidewalk. Cassie made the split-second decision to help the woman instead of pursuing her assailant and got to work like she was a trained nurse rather than a homemaker. She applied pressure to the wound and fished what looked like a very primitive flare gun out of a small satchel I hadn't noticed she was wearing. I wasn't sure the woman would last long enough for someone to see the flare and find us, but almost as soon as the flares were in the sky, Gabriel showed up.

"What's wrong?" he asked, ready to check her for wounds before seeing the woman.

"We need to help her." For the first time, I heard fear in Cassie's voice, as she looked into the fading blue eyes of the woman, before I was back in the room with Embry and present day Gabriel...

I could tell that this was one of the times I acted things out from the slits in the curtain and the way the guys were holding on to things I must have knocked over.

"Did you get him?" Embry asked, looking shocked.

"He ran away, but Cassie stayed to help a woman. She was bleeding so much I don't know if you were able to do anything other than make sure she didn't die alone," I shared, looking to Gabriel.

"She died in my arms a few hours later," he agreed somberly. "But they caught the man who did it from scratch marks on his face and puncture wounds in his arms."

"These are badass gloves." I tried to give them a smile, focusing on Cassie instead of the woman in the blue dress. My ancestor was the type of woman who wore such delicate gloves to conform to society, yet fitted them with deadly weapons.

"I believe they were her wedding gift from Allan." Gabriel pointed to the Roman numerals at the wrist, then opened another chest, steering me away from Cassie's failed rescue attempt.

The chest was full of jewelry, and there was an entire box filled with pictures in frames that must have been too painful for them to keep in the house after she died.

We unanimously decided on the gloves, which represented both her family and the fighter in her. We found a Ziploc bag to carry them in, and I snatched a few of the weapons that looked like they would still work.

After we ate a dinner of leftovers from the freezer, I went upstairs to the bedrooms. I walked past my room, but paused outside Clara's. I was used to knocking when the door was closed.

It looked just like I remembered, with a few extra teddies and trinkets from the beach. Clara didn't know I would come here, so it wasn't like she left me a note or a clue to tell me she was okay, but physically, it calmed me down to be close to her. I grabbed her biggest stuffed animal – a giant panda with a cape – and held him in my arms before lying back on the bed. As I looked up at the ceiling Sam decorated with glow-in-the-dark stickers of the solar system, my heart stopped pounding, my breathing slowed, and the tension I hadn't realized I was holding all over released.

We used to sit like this on rainy days, telling stories until her dad inevitably came up, pretending to be the tickle monster, and told us we had to seize the day, even if it was dark and cloudy outside.

"I nearly had a heart attack when you weren't in your room." Gabriel pulled me from a memory as he came into Clara's room and sat on the bed beside me.

"I'm sorry."

"You need to stop apologizing." I could hear the smile in his voice, but we were both looking at the ceiling.

"That'll probably never happen." I sighed.

"Lucy..." He was tentative, which made me feel like I didn't want to know what he was about to say.

"Yeah?" I gave him the permission he was waiting for.

"Sam didn't die so you could give up."

My first instinct was to turn and look at him in shock and anger, but I could feel the burn of tears and did not want to let him see that. Instead, I took a deep breath and let it out slowly, trying not to make a sound. I didn't know if Gabriel had more to say or if that was the extent of his attempt, but I stayed there, staring at the ceiling, trying to breathe.

I knew he was right, that I had to stop blaming myself for the things I did to save myself, and for the people I came from.

I was taking another deep breath when Gabriel reached over to take my hand in his. There were a million things he could have said, but none of them would say more than he already had.

CHAPTER EIGHT

W e left at the crack of dawn, but I was up long before then. I switched some clothes from my bag for the ones from my closet, mostly pants instead of shorts and dresses, and added some warm sweaters. I snuck into the master bedroom to take one of Deanna's scarves, then waited for the guys downstairs.

We walked along the boardwalk in the dark, with the sun coming up as we drove away. I had taken a pair of Sam's sunglasses, so I matched the guys in that respect, although none of us needed them this early in the morning. It garnered me a smile from Embry, who turned on the radio and sang along. I wasn't there yet, but I was trying.

THEY DID THEIR DETOURS, which I will never understand, so it was late afternoon by the time we got to the plantation. We stopped by the meadow, where the burnt line of grass and trees greeted us.

"I guess no one's been since I burnt it down?" We all stared through the windows, assessing the damage.

"I believe I was the one who threw the Molotov cocktails. You can claim the forest, but the plantation house is all me," Embry took a shot at me and got a smile in return. I would never have imagined smiling over arson before, especially not burning down a house that had been in my family for generations.

Gabriel drove slowly over the lawn, stopping in front of the garage, where the crispy remnants of the grey box told me the security system was down. The house looked slightly damaged from the outside, where you could see it caught fire, but a layer of reinforced steel stopped most of the flames.

"You were right about the tungsten," Embry told Gabriel.

"It's not steel?"

"A combination. It held up pretty good in some places." Gabriel took a critical eye to the structure, determining whether it was safe for us to go in. "Careful," he cautioned.

"Do you guys have anything in mind for Rosie? Something she treasured?" I looked from one to the other. Gabriel still looked guilty over not returning her affections, but no matter how much Beth was Embry's true love, there was no doubt in my mind that he had loved Rosalind, and still felt the sting of his unrequited feelings.

"I think her stuff is in the bunker," Gabriel ventured.

"I thought the bunker was only for people and dangerous books?"

"It's like Embry's." Gabriel shrugged.

I nodded. It was a room for things they didn't want to lose.

"A lot of the paintings and original decor were hers, but there was a box with her jewelry and trinkets that we moved to the safe as soon as they put it in," Embry shared.

WE WENT DOWN to the basement, which was the least damaged part of the house. The guys watched while I tried four times to get into the bunker. It required my blood, the code, and turning the knob a bunch of different ways, even without the computer system.

Once we got in, Gabriel went straight for a small, wooden box with carvings of roses on the sides, and 'My Darling Rosie' etched on the top.

I judged our potential items based on how easy they would be to carry, but they were trying to find a balance between things that meant the world to Rosie, and nothing to them. We didn't know what would remain of the objects once the spell was done with them.

"How about this?" I found a brooch wrapped in a lace handkerchief with 'R.G.' stitched into the corner of the fabric.

"It was her husband, Roger's. He gave her the brooch as well," Embry told me, but there was a look to him.

"You see something better?" I wasn't alive anywhere near the same time as her, so none of it meant anything to me, but I'd seen her wearing the brooch in a memory.

"One night when I was here, there was a fire. It was in the kitchen, and we put it out quickly, but just to be safe, we evacuated everyone from the house. Molly took a picture of Roger with her, but the only keepsake Rosalind took was that." Embry pointed to a piece of black fabric that felt like silk and held something heavy.

"A pebble?" Rock would have been my first guess, but it was much too smooth.

"I never knew Rosie to carry rocks." Gabriel cocked his head to the side, as curious as I was.

I removed the silk and found a clear block of what looked like a dandelion floating in… plastic?

"A flower?" I turned to Gabriel to see if he shared my confusion, but he had the stiffest upper lip I'd ever seen, his eyes focused on the block until he turned to Embry. The look he shot him was reminiscent of the previous centuries when they hated each other. If it meant this much to the two of them, it was probably emotional gold for Rosalind.

I brought it close to Gabriel, half-offering it, half-asking if I could use it, before the rest of the world slipped away...

I was in the plantation's foyer, but they set it up as a makeshift hospital for wounded soldiers of the war of independence, including Gabriel, who was lying in a bed watching Rosalind. It was weird because I wasn't inside anyone. I was intruding on the moment, like a fly on the wall.

Gabriel wasn't observing Rosie as a stalker, or as someone infatuated with her would; he was trying to solve a mystery. He perked up and strained to see when she moved her hair to rub her neck, but he slumped down, disappointed, when she let it fall again. He was trying to see if she had the crescent moon birthmark, and she wasn't making it easy.

I moved over to sit on the edge of his bed, taking advantage of my non-existence in this moment to take in every detail. His eyes were less dark than the Gabriel I knew, but every bit as intense. There was something hopeful about him, like he knew this wasn't Annabelle, but maybe she could be.

It was either a while after he first arrived, or he died here and regenerated, because his wounds were non-existent as he crept to the windows. Molly, Rosalind's daughter, was in the yard, picking flowers and placing them in a small wicker basket.

Gabriel was back in the bed before a doctor came in to check on him, but no one questioned him when he said they already changed his bandages. He was an excellent liar, but something about the way he pressed his lips together told me it wasn't the truth.

"I got them!" Molly rushed into the room, enthralled to be spending time with Gabriel, especially to be of use to him rather than an annoyance he tolerated.

"These are beautiful, Molly. Absolutely perfect." He beamed at her and her entire face lit up. I could tell he had experience with children, probably from Margaret, but there was also something holding him back. Some apprehension he was trying to hide, that Molly did not pick up on, but I did. Like he was afraid of her.

"How do you make them stay together?" Molly asked, trying to tie a knot between two flowers.

"Like this." Gabriel demonstrated, folding the stems as I had only ever seen with palm leaves. He finished a necklace, then let Molly put it over his head.

"You can't take it off now," she warned.

"I wouldn't dream of it," he assured her. "Now you try."

She made a solid attempt, Gabriel made an adjustment, then she quickly figured it out.

"You can start one for mama," she suggested when he was just watching her.

"Excellent idea." He worked slowly so Molly could help add the finishing touches once she was satisfied with her own.

"Can you tie mine?" She asked.

"It would be my pleasure."

He finished tying the stems together like a clasp just as Rosalind came in to check on him, or more likely make sure her daughter wasn't bothering him.

"Mama!" Molly ran over to show her mother the necklace she made.

"Wow, that's beautiful sweetheart." Rosie looked from her daughter to Gabriel, wondering what kind of man enjoyed making flower necklaces with a little girl. I could tell that she liked it. A lot.

"It was Gabriel's idea. We made you one too."

"This is for me?" Rosie asked, her hand pressed to her chest and her eyebrows raised. It was the way I overreacted to things for Clara, but I think she was genuinely touched.

"Don't worry, I didn't see any bugs in it." Gabriel gave her a smile as she turned around and pulled her hair out of the way, letting him tie the necklace for her. His breath caught and I don't think he could help himself as he traced the mark with his fingers. It was exactly like mine, like the dolls, down to the freckles in the crescent that looked like stars.

"Is something wrong?" Rosalind asked, snapping him out of his reverie and reminding him of his task. It would thoroughly creep me out *if some guy caressed the back of my neck like that, but she looked like she was just as lost in the moment as he was.*

"No, of course not." He gave no explanation for touching her in what definitely looked like a sensual way, but she didn't ask for one either...

"THE FLOWER IT IS." I tried to get up and act like it was normal for me to pass out and wake up on the ground, which it kind of was lately.

"Where did you go?" Just like the bedroom in New Orleans, this time it was Gabriel's turn to be nervous about how much I saw.

"When you gave them to her."

"And she felt…" Gabriel tried to find the words to ask what he wanted to know, but it was mostly to torture himself for hurting her.

"I don't know what she was feeling," I admitted.

"You were in me?" His eyes widened in horror.

"No, it was weird. I was just in the room. Like I tapped into the moment rather than a memory."

"You saw it all from above, or…" Embry was curious.

"No, I could walk around. It's just weird when I can see myself instead of being myself," I tried to explain. "Rosie was there last time too."

"It happened before?" Gabriel asked. "You saw another moment?"

"The other one was a memory, I think." I based my assumption on how this time it happened when I touched the flower block, whereas last time I was touching them. I wrapped the flower into Roger's handkerchief instead of the silk, thus representing her husband, her daughter, and Gabriel; the three people she cared about most. The guys were looking at me expectantly, so I elaborated. "It was of the two of you arguing. It happened when you were fighting and I tried to separate you, so I don't know whose memory it was. Maybe both."

"You get them at will then," Embry concluded.

"No, I did not want to see what I saw," I argued. "Is this all the spell books? We should grab them and get to the manor before dark," I suggested when it looked like they were both going to ask for more details about their memory.

"I was thinking we should get something smaller than the dagger for Annabelle. Preferably something that never belonged to anyone else." Gabriel put his own curiosity aside for me.

"Like what?" The plantation was her family home once upon a time, so there were lots of family heirlooms and things that must have belonged to her, but it went through many renovations, and I wasn't aware of any secret jewelry boxes of hers. Then again, I never knew about Rosie's.

"It is October…" He looked pointedly at me, then down to my neck.

"What do… the locket?" I clued in, bringing my hand to the moonstone necklace I was wearing instead of the locket my grandmother used to make me wear around Halloween.

"Evelyn didn't tell you?" Embry read my confusion.

"She did not," I agreed. A common theme for everyone and everything in my life these days.

"It was Annabelle's. She had it with her when she died."

"She was wearing it when they burnt her?" I involuntarily recoiled. It was one thing to have Beth's old ring in my bag, but I wore the necklace that touched her searing flesh for months over the years, if not more.

"It was untouched by the flames. We were told to give it to Margaret, and your ancestors have passed it down ever since."

"Is it something Henry gave to her?" I asked, even though the answer might make my skin crawl.

"No, she had it the first day I met her. Minus the rope and hair," Gabriel assured me.

"Is that why it smells so bad?" I assumed the rope and hair were inside the seal.

"You're exaggerating. It's a little musty, but hair and twine don't smell like rotting flesh."

"Did all the others wear it too?" I tried to remember if I was wearing it in any of the memories.

"We had more control over that when they were children. As in Margaret wore it and made her daughter wear it and so on. It would disappear for a generation or two, then Henry would resurface, and it wasn't just a silly superstition anymore."

"But my mom never wore it."

"Not that I saw. I remember Corinne wore it every single day until she passed it on to her daughter, who wasn't as interested."

"I'll go get it," I relented.

"I'll pack up any books or things that might be useful." Embry picked up one of the magic books we hid down here when we left. What we were originally coming here for. Magic books were more useful when you had someone who could do magic, and we needed all the help we could get.

GABRIEL FOLLOWED me upstairs in case someone showed up, or the building collapsed on me, but I also got the feeling he wanted to say something.

"It wasn't the fight that made you guys ignore each other this summer." But Eric had filled me in that their fight was about feelings Gabriel might have for me, rather than Embry's feelings for Annabelle, as I had originally assumed.

He looked at me, surprised. There was a flash of him wondering how much I knew about that fight, but I didn't want to talk about it, and his face told me he didn't either.

"Give me a decade. Or at least a century," he teased. The smile implied he wasn't so concerned, at least not now that he knew it wasn't the one about me.

"1770s." I shrugged, going through the hooks on the wall of my closet. I was a lot less good at wearing the locket consistently now that Grams and Mrs. Boyd weren't reminding me. Sam would say something if he saw it, but he had an out of sight, out of mind mentality when it came to Grams' eccentricities, so I kept it at the plantation instead of the manor.

"We fought all the time back then."

"Are you afraid of all children, or just Molly?" I brought us back to my most recent memory, rather than the one where he told Embry we merely look like a woman we can never live up to.

"Afraid of Molly?" He raised an eyebrow, but played along.

"The entire time you were making necklaces with her, you were trying to bury your fear, or…"

"Pretend I didn't care," he understood. "Margaret was easy, I could just pretend she was mine. I'm sure Embry did the same, but I never wanted to get close to another child after that. I watched Margaret grow up, but no matter how old she got, when she died, she was still… I didn't want to go through that again. But Molly was… I pretended I couldn't care less, that I was giving her projects to keep her out of my hair, but after generations without letting anyone in… she was curious and caring and innocent and everything I didn't know I needed."

I digested the information, of him sharing his vulnerability with me, and took a chance.

"Then it's caring that you're afraid of?" I teased with a smile instead of dwelling on how lonely it must be to watch everyone you care about die, then have to keep going.

"Terrible things often happen when I do. People get hurt," he agreed, choosing to keep it honest, rather than the out I gave him. "With Rosalind, I was so focused on pointing out how she wasn't Annabelle that I didn't notice the dozens of ways she was amazing in her own right. She was strong, selfless in caring for her patients, a devoted mother… she would light up a room no matter how dark it appeared to be…"

"Why are you telling me this?"

His eyes were looking at me with that intensity that made my heart beat faster and my cheeks flush.

"Being afraid doesn't stop me from caring. It stops me from letting the other person know, which ultimately causes more pain for everyone." He found my eyes and his guilt told me he might know exactly what memory I saw.

It was just the two of us in the closet, and he was being vulnerable and looking at me in a way that made me want to move closer, but my heart was beating a mile a minute and I was terrified of what might happen if I was wrong.

Just as I moved my hand closer to his, the locket shifted, and I was pulled away…

MY HEART SANK at being ripped from the moment, but I was definitely not expecting to be Annabelle, wrists tied to a post behind my back as the ground beneath me was burning. Inside I was screaming, but Annabelle stood tall and looked ahead, not letting it get to her, even as the flames licked her feet. Gabriel and Embry were in the crowd, taking it a lot harder than Annabelle was. It burned, and I wanted to struggle to get free, to use my magic to freeze the flames… anything. Instead, I stood there, stoic and strong, the locket around my neck the only thing that wasn't on fire…

"WAS IT THE LOCKET?" Gabriel asked, horrified.

There were a million memories the locket could hold, but he knew which one it would bring. I nodded and shivered, not because I was cold, but I needed to get the feeling of being burned alive – for a second time this week – out of my skin.

"Come on, let's bring you home." He wrapped an arm around me and led me back outside.

<h1 style="text-align:center">CHAPTER NINE</h1>

I stayed in the car with the doors locked and the key in the ignition while the guys went to make sure the manor was safe. It looked exactly the same from the outside, but it felt empty and cold. It always seemed like that on the surface, because we were four people living in a ginormous building with old heating systems, but the inside was usually warm and cozy.

After about thirty minutes of reading a book on the laws of magic, Embry came out to escort me and the car inside. He had me activate all the alarms while he carried the rest of the books from the bunker into the kitchen.

"Should we go to my mom's room?" Part of me wanted to stay as long as it took for word to get out that we were here, so Clara and Deanna would come and I could see them for real, but the bigger part needed us to get what we came for and leave as soon as possible. I couldn't be responsible for any more dreadful things happening to them.

"I'll start supper," Gabriel offered.

"I'll go on the adventure." Embry whisked me upstairs. I spent my childhood with people bribing me with trips to her room, so calling it an adventure was accurate.

Once inside, all I could see was my father telling her he was basically paid to sleep with her because Henry was worried a teenager dying of cancer would let the Owens line die out otherwise. I shivered at the thought.

"Did you have something in mind?" Embry asked, bringing me back to the task at hand.

"Everything I found in here as a kid was magical and meant the world to me, because it belonged to her."

"I think I remember you carrying around a doily for days until Mrs. Boyd told you what it was."

"I blame everyone who didn't give me more to go on." I meant it in the sense that I wish I knew more about her. Not that I blamed the Boyds.

"I'll tell you as much as I know about whatever you find." He gave me free rein, but I didn't know where to start, or how much he actually knew about her.

"If you had to pick something in here, what would you choose?" I turned it on him.

"You." He smiled. "You were what meant the most to her in the entire world."

"I would rather not resort to human sacrifices, but I'm open to other suggestions." I looked around. "None of this is familiar except from my own memories of exploring the room when I was really good, or when bad things happened to me," I pointed out.

"How do you picture her?"

"I have the actual memories of a woman with a scarf around her head, who is scared and weak, but also fighting. Who smiles whenever she knows I'm looking. Then I have the ones I make up from pictures of her when she is young, happy, and alive. The thing I had that most reminded me of her was the blanket, which I now know was Brian's."

"Marilyn didn't wear fancy jewelry, and I don't remember many trinkets. She had a lot of stuffed animals when she was in the hospital, but she usually gave them all away before she came home and got new ones for her next stay."

"Did she wear not-fancy jewelry? A Cracker Jack box ring would do if it meant something to her." The plastic ring from Clara was the object I was most attached to at the moment. I fished around without going too deep. It felt like I was intruding this time, rather than discovering more about my mom.

"She made jewelry." Embry got one of those sad smiles from when he remembered something about someone he lost. "The last one she sent me was one of those wish bracelets that you tie around your ankle."

"And when it breaks the wish comes true." I made them with Clara once.

"I don't think that's how it worked," he argued.

"Did it have beads?" I could vaguely remember a picture of me eating something from my mom's wrist.

"She put my initials on mine. Her wish was to keep everyone safe, so she told me it would protect me as long as I wore it."

"Do you still have it?" Even if it didn't belong to her, she probably put a lot of herself into it.

"I wore it every day for years, while Gabriel left his in a box at Terrence's. I lost mine, and it was like I committed a terrible offence. I don't think she ever forgave me."

"At least he still has his." I gave him a knowing smile.

"If memory serves, hers was always pink or purple."

"Let's find it."

We looked on all the exposed surfaces, then ventured into drawers and boxes. I was familiar with the lower drawers of her standing bureau, the only ones I could reach as a tiny kid. I was exploring the top ones when Embry exclaimed, "Found it!"

"M.E.O.," I read. My mom's name was Marilyn, and we had a history of keeping our maternal surname of Owens. "Elizabeth?" I guessed.

"Helen and I might have told your Grams a few stories," he agreed.

"Any thoughts on Suzanne?" I asked of my middle name.

"She liked the name?" He let me know it didn't mean anything to him, then dropped the bracelet in my hand so I could add it to the other objects, but the moment it touched me...

"Are you making a wish?" Brian asked as my mom tied the bracelet around her ankle. We were in a hospital, but she didn't look sick like I remembered her, just a little tired.

"I never use those rules," she argued.

"The conventional rules that apply to all wish bracelets?" He came over and took her in his arms, looking at her like she was his entire world, though the setting definitely made him uncomfortable.

"If it needs to break to release your wish, you would just be super rough with it until it did, which is stupid."

"What are your rules?" He kissed the top of her head, and she closed her eyes, her entire body relaxing.

"Well..." She took out another bracelet and tied it around his wrist. "As long as you're wearing this, it will keep you safe." She gave him a smile. She knew how unrelated the two were, but this wasn't her first rodeo, and little kids were quick to believe in magic bracelets. Especially if they got to go home while other kids in the ward never made it out of the operating room.

"Then you are never allowed to take yours off."

"Why not?" She bit her bottom lip, but he didn't play along to her fishing. He got serious.

"Because I can't lose you," he said with an intensity that had me taking a closer look at his eyes, but they were green. Like mine.

"I'm not going anywhere." She took him in her arms...

"Bad memory?" Embry asked when I woke up in his arms.

"Happy memory. Evil person," I brushed it off and stood up with a sigh.

"Care to tell me exactly what you saw?" All I'd told them so far was that my dad was not a nice person.

"Not particularly." I wrapped my arms around myself and walked back to the bureau, more out of habit than anything else. "I'm trying to focus on nurture over nature. And who knows, maybe my mom—" I picked up a picture as I was talking and recognized it as the blurry one I've always had of my father, only this one was perfectly clear, of Brian holding me in his arms and smiling so much he was crying...

"How did you get in here?" my mom asked Brian.

"Sam let me in," he admitted, looking guilty and heartbroken.

"How cunning of you. Manipulating a ten-year-old." He was upsetting her, but she made no effort to get him out.

"I brought this for you. Well, for the baby. I don't know if it's a boy, or a girl, but my grandmother made it for me when I was born, and she insists it was blessed and will keep the baby safe. I figured it can't hurt." He tried to hand her my blankie, but she didn't take it.

"What do you want?"

"I need to tell you what happened," he pleaded, like his life depended on it.

"Yes, well, since you told me to have an abortion, I don't really care what you have to say. Which is why I told you never to come back here." I could feel how much she loved him, still, but she didn't know what I knew. Yet.

"I need you to know why I said that."

"Because you were young, you had your whole life ahead of you and you didn't want to waste it being tied down to some girl you slept with a few times." She used her vulnerability as a weapon, the words slicing into him.

"Even if you don't believe a word I say to you today, even if you want to keep believing I just wasn't ready to be a father, you have to know that you were so much more than that to me. That you

mean the world to me. I will love you until the day I die," he promised.

"How could I know that when you told me to kill our baby? Knowing that it was probably the only chance I would ever get, and that the thing I have wanted more than anything my entire life was to be a mom?"

"I had to try and convince you not to. You should have had an abortion." He didn't even try to deny it. "But you were the one who decided that my telling you not to have the baby meant that I wouldn't want to stick around if you did."

"I didn't want you anywhere near her." She had tears in her eyes, but she looked at him with pure hatred.

"Her?" I could see his brain working, trying to imagine what I looked like, whose nose I had, what hair color...

"I would love to tell you you have a daughter, but she's mine." I think the hurt in her voice affected him more than her words.

"Can I see her?"

I was forced to watch the part of the memory I heard at the campus library. As if once wasn't bad enough, I got to listen to my father tell my mother about the man who paid him to hang out with her, who was so happy when she got pregnant, because it meant she would continue the line before her cancer killed her.

"He sent you to sleep with me?" My mom was horrified, and I was more than ready to get back to the present, away from this conversation.

"He only told me after he realized that we had. It's not like he told me to do it, he was just happy when we did. That's when he explained it all to me. He told me he was worried because you had cancer, and you didn't go out much, and he thought you might die without leaving a child to ensure there would be more copies." Each word disgusted him more than the last. I think he hated himself as much as we did.

"Then why did you tell me to have an abortion? Was it some mind game to free yourself and make sure I would keep her?" My mom was way more clear-headed than me, actually taking the time to process what he was telling her.

"When he told me why I was doing it... I couldn't. I mean, yes, he

paid for my school and dorm and asked me to hang out with you, but you weren't some stranger... I didn't mind because I liked you. And then I really liked you. And then I loved you. And that's when he told me the truth. As soon as I knew why he was so interested in you, I came here to tell you, but then you told me you were pregnant and I know I should have handled it better, or explained why, but... The point is, I told you to have an abortion not because I don't love you or wasn't already in love with that baby, but because some day, that little girl, or her little girl, will be used in his messed-up game, and I wanted to protect her from that."

"This is crazy. You're not making sense," my mom argued, not wanting it to be true.

"I know, it sounds crazy. It's ridiculous, and maybe it isn't true, but he believes it. And some day, he will come after you and our daughter," he emphasized the 'our' to let her know he hadn't given up on it.

THEY WENT TO FIND GRAMS, who not only believed it, but looked destroyed by it. She told Brian to leave her house, then went to make phone calls.

"Her name is Lucy," my mom said once they were in her bedroom to get his coat. "Lucine Suzanne Owens."

I thought he might be upset about the Owens, but his face lit up. "Suzanne?" he asked.

"Your grandmother was sweet and strong and wasn't afraid to tell it like it is."

"The last thing I ever wanted was to hurt you, Marilyn. You are my heart."

"I want to believe you, but I don't think I can trust you." She looked torn.

"I'll just have to spend the rest of my life proving it to you."

"Your blanket," she said when he left it on her bureau.

"It's Lucy's now," he argued. They shared a look that broke my heart.

"Do you want to hold her? Just once," my mom offered.

"More than anything." He followed her to the bassinet, beaming when

she put me in his arms. He held me close, like he wanted to protect me from everything.

A camera flash made him turn to my mother, who was shaking a Polaroid. "Smile in this one," she requested, so he obliged.

"What was that for?"

"One day she'll ask about you, and I want to have something to show her."

"Hopefully she won't have to ask." There was a moment where they looked to each other, both of them wanting that, but my mom couldn't admit to it, and he could see he had a long way to go to get there...

"HAVE you considered hanging out around beds and chairs rather than open spaces?" Embry must have caught me, because I was on the bed rather than on the ground, but the memories never came so close together before.

"He wasn't evil." I ignored his suggestion.

"Your father?" he guessed, going off the picture in my hands.

"I mean, he was very flawed and made some awful decisions, but he loved her."

"Everyone did." He gave me a sad smile.

"Back at the library, the memory I saw made it seem like Henry paid a boy to woo my mom and sleep with her so she could continue the line."

"That's disgusting."

"I know."

"What really happened?"

"Henry saw that my mom liked him, so he offered him a job, and to pay his tuition and stuff. It was all just a ploy for him to be close to her. He tried to tell my mom as soon as he found out, but she was pregnant and didn't take it well when he told her to have an abortion."

"I'm sorry." Embry was horrified.

"You're upset at how close he was to us, how involved he was when you had no clue Henry was behind it... I'm relieved that he didn't orchestrate my birth, he just facilitated it."

"Is that why you were so convinced you were evil and didn't deserve to be saved?"

"One of many reasons," I agreed. I put the picture back in the bureau and found a faded newspaper clipping about a young man drowning when his car drove off a bridge. They were unable to identify the body, but given the fact that my mom kept it, I had a pretty good idea who it was.

EMBRY FOLLOWED me closely on the staircase, ready to catch me if I slipped away again, but I remained in the present. We had a surprisingly okay supper, but it was an emotionally exhausting day for me, and I was ready to go to bed.

"Now we have all the things..."

"Let's stay a couple of days, make a game plan, then go off on your suicide mission?" Embry suggested.

"It's not really suicide if it's inevitable. And the purpose of the mission is to prevent it from happening."

I could tell he was about to argue, but we all froze as the kitchen door opened behind me. I brought my hands up as I turned, terrified but ready to go down fighting. Thank God my instinct was to freeze rather than explode, because not only did I recognize the man frozen in front of us, I loved him with my whole heart.

"Sam?!?"

CHAPTER TEN

"I have to unfreeze him," I said for what felt like the millionth time this evening. The guys tied Sam up using zip ties so he couldn't hurt us using human means, but they were reluctant to discover what magic he might have.

"Not until we know what he is and have a plan," Gabriel argued.

"He's Sam," I repeated. This certainty was probably why they didn't trust me to unfreeze him. "And if he isn't, our best way of finding that out is to talk to him."

"Or to whip up a truth serum." I'm pretty sure Embry was joking, but it was one of the potions Ingrid taught me over the summer.

"I know we all learnt our lesson with the faeries, but I don't think you could hurt someone who looked like Sam, no matter who he really is," Gabriel said delicately.

"I could freeze him again."

"We're not getting anywhere with him like this," he reluctantly agreed, exchanging a look with Embry. "I want you to freeze him the second he says anything that gives you the slightest hesitation," he warned me.

"Okay," I agreed, then waited for him to nod before unfreezing Sam.

I wasn't worried, because this had to be him, but if it wasn't, the guys were right. Something evil that looked like Sam was better than no Sam at all, as long as he didn't try to kill us.

"Lucy!" His greeting sounded like he was upset with me, until his brain caught up to his new physical predicament and he looked down at his zip-tied hands and feet. "What the—" Confusion and anger mixed into his unfinished question, which was unlike Sam from before, but fitting for someone who was on the run and recently died because of me.

"We tied you up so we could make sure it's you," I explained, trying to take a step towards him, but Gabriel put his arm out to stop me. He and Embry were standing on either side of me, but slightly in front, so they just had to take a step towards each other if things went south and they would form a wall between our presumed enemy and me.

"Because I died." He let out a breath that held a million emotions, but every single one made me feel guilty.

"We've had our share of fake you's, so we have to be cautious." I tried to act normal, but every inch of me wanted to run into his arms.

"Fake me's?" He had the tiniest trace of his crooked smile. He understood this wasn't an interrogation for knowledge. It was to see if my big brother was in there somewhere.

"There's a fairy in New Orleans that lures people who are mourning a loss into the swamps. We didn't know they did it by looking like the person you've lost," I explained.

"I tried to kill you?" He was concerned, even though I was clearly alive and well in front of him.

"You did," I agreed.

"I'm so sorry, Luce. I wanted to contact you and let you know, but I didn't know how to do that without risking your safety."

"Because it really is you, isn't it?" I could tell the guys weren't convinced yet, but I was ready to untie him and celebrate.

"That, or I'm dreaming."

"What happened to you?"

"I remember dying, and you rushing to me before everything went dark. I was dead, I guess, but I wasn't anywhere until I woke up. Like a vampire, only I was me. I was starving for actual food, not blood, but my main priority was finding you."

"Where did you wake up?" Gabriel tested his story.

"In a large pit. There were fingernail markings that told me I wasn't the first to climb out, but there was still a body at the bottom when I left. By the time I figured out where I was and got to the motel, police officers and caution tape surrounded it. I couldn't just go up to them covered in blood and ask about their investigation, so I found a squad car and hid in the bushes behind it until I made sure on the radio that they hadn't found any teenage girls."

"Why didn't you go home?" Embry asked.

"They found me once, so I didn't want to risk them coming after my girls. I've been trying to keep an eye on them while keeping my distance. I've been here since they moved in with Deanna's father."

"How are they?" I asked.

"Deanna's doing a good job of making it seem like a fun adventure, but Clara's getting to be too smart for her own good. They're safe, but they're worried."

My entire body was stiff from holding my arms by my side and preventing myself from going to him. I looked to the guys in an 'are you satisfied?' way, but they still weren't convinced.

"Ask something only Sam would know," Embry suggested.

"What's the secret ingredient in your mom's French toast?"

"Vanilla."

"What was your dad's favorite color?"

"Orange."

"What did Clara call me before she could say Lucy?"

"Lala."

I fired all the questions in quick succession and Sam answered them without missing a beat, so I turned to Embry, who nodded. I think he just meant for me to go close, but I used my powers to break the zip ties so Sam could wrap his arms around me and hopefully make me feel safe, as if this summer hadn't happened.

"What was that?" Sam asked when he realized that although his instincts kicked in and he was holding me now, he'd been tied up a moment ago.

"I really haven't been okay," I said before burying my head in his chest.

I COULD TELL that the guys wanted to give us a minute to catch up, but they also weren't one hundred percent certain they trusted Sam to be alone with me, so they let us sit at the table while they made tea and coffee for everyone.

"Did you know you were Gifted?" I asked, no longer taking anything for granted.

"I had no idea. I thought I was in hell, or purgatory at first, until I realized there was a more likely explanation."

"Do you know what your Gift is?" I focused the conversation on him, though I could tell he wanted to ask a million questions about me.

"I think I was overlooked growing up..." His hand literally disappeared in front of me.

"Invisibility?"

"I was hoping for flying, but I'll take it," he teased. "Speaking of superpowers..."

"I'm not a superhero," I argued.

"Did we fail?" He asked of his worst fear being realized.

"No, I'm a witch. Apparently. Annabelle and Beth were too."

"That's..."

"Not as fun as it sounds," I said before he could tell me how awesome it was. "I found out about it when I accidentally pulverized someone, then it took forever before I could control it enough to not attack anyone who got close."

We discussed it further before the guys brought us warm beverages and we had a lighter conversation to catch up on more pleasant topics.

SLEEPING in my own bed didn't make me feel like I was safe and at home, it felt weird. So, when I woke up at dawn with a splitting headache, I gave up on sleep and went down to make myself a tea.

It was steeping on the counter when Sam walked in, looking apprehensive at first, but then his entire body relaxed.

"I was worried it was a dream." He came and took me in his arms. We weren't necessarily a hugging family before, at least not every time we saw each other, but I mirrored his sentiment.

"I didn't want to ruin last night, but... how's the Big Bad?" He asked, turning on the coffee machine.

"He's..." I let out a deep breath, searching for the best way to explain it all to him. "The Big Bad's name is Henry, and he was married to Annabelle, which makes him my ancestor. She found the Prophecy and left him, so he has been hunting us down ever since."

"At least you got some answers," he offered me the tiniest of silver linings.

"I can also promise that Clara's life will be back to normal before she graduates high school," I said as if it was another positive in this messed up situation.

"What do you mean?"

"I only have to avoid Henry for the next ten years, because no matter what we do, the Bearers of the Crescent Moon die at twenty-eight."

"That's... there has to be something we can do," he argued.

"There's a spell. So far it looks like we just have to collect a few objects and random ingredients, nothing scary, but I feel like there has to be a catch."

"If there's a spell to make you not die, we're using it." He left no room for discussion.

"That's the plan, I just don't think it can really be as easy as putting rings and flowers in a bowl."

"Rings and flowers?"

"I need objects from my mother, my father, and every bearer of the crescent moon who came before me." I sighed.

"How are you going to do that? You don't know who your father is and—"

"We got the last piece last night," I cut him off, not ready to get into that story. "I have my father's baby blanket and my mom's bracelet, then I have Annabelle's locket, Rosalind's flower rock thing, Cassie's weaponized gloves, and Beth's family ring."

"You found your father?" He was more concerned than excited for me, probably wondering why I didn't mention it last night.

"He was this guy named Brian Sherwood. I'm pretty sure he's dead, though."

"He taught me the Thriller dance," Sam told me after thinking about it. I forgot that in the memory, Sam was the one who let him in.

"He was a nice guy?"

"I liked him. He came over a lot for about a year, and then he came back once when you were a baby. Your mom had told me he was never coming back, so I was thrilled when he showed up, but it was just the one time."

"Yeah, he… it's complicated," I brushed it off, but when he gave me another concerned look, I reluctantly agreed to tell him later.

"How did you get stuff from the others?" He poured himself some coffee.

"What others?"

"The other Bearers of the Crescent Moon," he used my language. "Unless you only need the last four?"

"Annabelle was the first." As I said it, I realized I had absolutely nothing to back it up.

"She was the first that Gabriel and Embry met, the first to come to America… but she wasn't the first."

"I only have four dolls," I pointed out, but the references to the Prophecy implied it started long before Annabelle. Like five hundred years before she was born. And Sam clearly knew something I didn't.

"I commissioned the dolls." Embry came into the kitchen, his eyes on Sam, suggesting he was listening from the staircase. A thought confirmed by Gabriel following him in.

"Who told you there were others?" I asked Sam, who looked surprised that the guys didn't know.

"Genevieve."

I looked at him expectantly, but Embry and Gabriel clearly knew her.

"She kept a diary?" Embry asked.

"Letters to her husband."

"Who are we talking about?" I waited for one of them to fill me in.

"Cassie's mom died when she was very little, so her father hired Mrs. Lovell to take care of her. Her daughter, Genevieve, and Cassie were like sisters…" Embry started.

"She's the Gen who fought crimes with Cassie." Her name popped up frequently in the Chronicles.

"And she's *my* ancestor," Sam emphasized, as if to show that his family was interesting and went back generations as well.

"When your mom said her family had been looking after mine for a long time, she didn't mean just you and your dad."

"Martha's family has been linked to yours since roughly 1830," Gabriel shared.

I looked to Sam, wondering how many people I needed to

hunt down now, but also feeling betrayed by yet another thing he kept from me.

"I've had a lot of time in the house, and I wanted to find out more about being Gifted, so I went through my mother's old things. I don't know if I was nostalgic or if I needed to make sense of things, but Gen's letters were the only ones that mentioned anything supernatural."

"What did she say about us?" I counted myself as one of the Bearers.

"I can get the letters for you, but basically, she and Cassie went to England before Cassie's wedding, and they stumbled into someone who knew her. Or, you know, knew someone who looked like her."

"How many were there?" Embry asked.

"Cassie wanted to stay to find out, but she had the wedding."

"Go get the letters." Gabriel sighed.

"It didn't even occur to me about the other Bearers." I clenched my teeth and shook my head as Sam rushed up the stairs. We had nothing from anyone before Annabelle and her parents.

"How much do you know about them?" Embry asked me.

"There was a brief passage in a book Beth was reading. The oldest mention of someone being marked by the Crescent Moon was in 1148, and again with Talina and Zeke, who ruled from 1385 to 1460," I shared, knowing it wasn't much to go on. "What do we do?"

"If there were others… you saw the spell, we need something from every Bearer who came before you."

"In England?" I asked. "How do you know anything would even be there anymore?"

"We have to try." Gabriel had a lot more determination and confidence than me.

. . .

SAM CAME DOWNSTAIRS with a stack of letters, but they were fifty percent Gen missing her husband, forty-five percent praising Europe and its beautiful sights, with maybe five percent of it relevant to us. She never gave specifics, either because she didn't think he would care, or because she was keeping it a secret.

The letter with the most details was her second, sent a couple of days after their arrival. I was reading it out loud when I found myself living it instead…

"JUDITH! JUDITH!" A man ran across the street, trying to flag Cassandra and another woman down. He looked so happy to see her that he forgot himself and tried to take her in his arms, but as soon as he got too close for comfort, she hit him in the stomach with the rounded end of her umbrella.

"You don't remember me," he said, doubled over to clutch his stomach.

"No, I do not," she agreed. He intrigued her more than he scared her. "How do you think you know me?"

"My name is Alaric." He paused to see if it would jog her memory. "I was at your wedding."

"You're mistaken, Sir. I'm not from here and my fiancé—" Cassandra tried to be polite, but exchanged a glance with her friend, probably Genevieve.

"It was in 1560," he stopped her.

"And what did you call me?" She'd only met a handful of people who knew another Bearer, but none of them had mistaken her for someone else yet.

"Judith. But you're not her," he said sadly.

"I'm not. And I'm terribly sorry, but we're expected for dinner and—"

"Of course," he assured her. "Meet me tomorrow for lunch. My estate is just outside of London, one of those old ones that everyone knows where to find since it's been in the family for ages."

"I don't think I can. We're very busy." Cassie was nervous, but it wasn't about the stranger.

"Please?" The look he gave softened her.

"I'll see what I can do," she decided.

"Dawes Estate. I'll see you tomorrow." He gave her a smile, full of nostalgia, then let her continue on her way...

"HER NAME WAS JUDITH," I shared when I came back to them.

"Anything we can use to find her?" Embry asked.

"The man who recognized Cassie had an estate outside of London. He said it's been in his family for generations, so he might still be there."

"I guess we're going to London." Embry gave me fake enthusiasm.

THE GUYS PUT in a few calls to arrange our travel while I stayed back in the kitchen with Sam.

"I don't think I renewed my passport after the baby moon fell through," he told me.

"We probably don't need those. Last time I crossed the border with them, I was in the back of a pickup, surrounded by chicken and roosters."

"You must have loved that." He laughed at me.

"We do what we have to." I shrugged before getting serious. "You can't come with us."

"I'm already dead, Lucy. And I can do this." He made his body disappear to prove his point.

"Exactly. I've been living the past few months wracked with guilt because I thought I killed you. There is no way I could get over it twice."

"I don't think it's up to you."

"I think you got to be invisible because it lets you keep an eye on Deanna and Clara without getting them in danger. That's where you need to be."

"And who will make sure you don't follow fairies into ponds over there?"

"I learnt my lesson. And you know Gabriel and Embry won't let anything happen to me."

"They're a lot friendlier than they used to be," he pointed out instead of agreeing to not come.

"They had a huge fight and eventually made up for everything."

"I'll make a deal with you. Promise me you'll come home and be at my daughter's graduation, then I'll let you go without me."

"Only if you promise you'll save my seat," I turned it on him, since neither of us could promise such things.

"I promise." He looked into my eyes, and even if it was fueled by hope, I believed him.

"I promise too."

"I'll hold you to it," he warned before we went to pack.

I SPENT the rest of the day sifting through the magic books, trying to find anything that could help us become more powerful before confronting Henry and his army. A lot of the books were more theoretical, but there were also a lot of spells with graphic images of what they did. If the goal was to torture Henry into admitting something, we would be golden, only I couldn't even look at the pictures without wanting to throw up, and it said it wasn't enough to hate someone, you had to want to see them suffer. Embry told me the books were mostly for research, or gifted to them by friends trying to be helpful, but I was really glad we found Kiara's cure, because the books were a major disappointment. There was a tiny passage in one book stating that the Bearers of the Crescent Moon are strongest during the Crescent Moon, but I felt like we could have figured that out for ourselves.

CHAPTER ELEVEN

We left before dawn the following morning, with Sam driving us. He could make anything he touched invisible, which was awesome, but also terrifying when the other cars couldn't see us. He only used it from the manor into town, where we could get lost in the crowd, but it was not an experience I wanted to repeat.

We drove into a secluded entrance of the Logan International Airport, with passports bearing other people's names. Sam took me in his arms and said, "I'll see you soon," before I watched him drive away, praying to God he was right.

I had most of my stuff in my backpack, except for Cassie's gloves and Annabelle's dagger, which Gabriel was holding on to while I went through the security line. We were away from prying eyes with only airport employees around us, but that also meant it would be very hard to get anything past them.

"When you guys said you were making arrangements, I thought you found another crop duster in a nearby field, not that we were flying on a private plane," I told Embry while returning my tiny bag of liquids into my backpack.

"Those aren't designed for transatlantic flights, and we're on a time crunch," he reminded me. It wasn't like there was anything that said we had to perform Kiara's Cure under the upcoming crescent moon, but since it was the only supermoon this year, we figured it couldn't hurt to aim for sooner rather than later. "We're also not on a private plane, this is just to avoid the crowded airport and board in anonymity."

"But it's a passenger plane?" I verified.

"You'll have a seat," he teased. Given previous modes of transportation, I wasn't reassured.

I looked back to Gabriel, to see how he was getting through with all the weapons we were bringing, but after a few words with the security guys, he handed them something I couldn't see. I tried to read the expression on the guard's face, but he brought Gabriel to a partitioned area.

"Did Gabriel just get arrested?" I asked Embry in a whisper, as a man in a suit went into the room as well. I'd expected him to buzz at the metal detector because of the shrapnel in his shoulder. He told me it was a hassle because he didn't have the scars that should go with that kind of wound, but Embry digging the tracker out of him should provide enough plausibility to let him through this time. He never mentioned anyone detaining him for it.

"I don't think so." Embry wasn't concerned.

"He just tried to bribe a security guard," I pointed out.

"When?" He looked back as if the moment would play out again for him.

"He opened his jacket and handed them something I couldn't see... how did you guys get us in here?"

"He just showed them his badge," Embry reassured me, but it didn't help.

"He thought he could get the dagger through with a fake cop badge?" I whispered. I didn't want the government to overhear me if Keisha was right and they bugged airports with microphones. That might explain his being brought into a different room. I knew Gabriel had been a soldier in lots of wars, and he did a short stint in a restaurant, but neither of those should allow him to board a plane with weapons.

"His badge is FBI, and it's real," Embry said like it wasn't a huge deal.

"And what, you're CIA?" I asked.

"Wouldn't you like to know," he teased before they let Gabriel out of the isolation area. He shook hands with the man in a suit, then caught up to us.

"What happened?" I asked him.

"We're good," he assured me.

THEY BROUGHT us to the plane on one of those trolley things and we boarded from a door in the back. There were two seats in that row for us, and another one in the last row, with the flight attendants.

"See you on the other side," Embry, who got on first, told me before making his way to the single seat, leaving me with Gabriel.

He put his seatbelt on, placed his arms on the armrests, and settled in for the flight. I put my seatbelt on, and was going to sit there quietly, but I wasn't good at keeping my curiosity to myself.

"You're FBI?" I turned to ask him in a whisper.

"A long time ago," he said loosely, looking around to make sure no one was listening to us. All the other passengers were following the safety briefing. "I've done lots of things," he reminded me.

"Was this during my lifetime?" I couldn't picture him wearing a suit with the earpiece, going to an office every day. Then again, it might explain some of his reluctance for talking and sharing. "Or did the guard just not look at the date?"

"Recently enough that I still have friends there who don't mind supplying the occasional badge for me. They'll also vouch for me whenever I get into one of these situations. They know I'm not about to bring a plane down, and they're used to not asking questions, so they'll cover for me with a fake op or justifying my need for personal protection," he said like it wasn't a huge deal.

"You must have been really good at it." I shrugged, putting my backpack under the seat as the flight attendant came over. I doubted high-ranking FBI officials had that many people they would lie like that for.

"It became something different from what I signed up for, but the guys who joined with me... even though I would never go back, I would do anything for them," he shared.

"You'll have to tell me about them some time. Or we can have them over for dinner once all of this is settled. You can share war stories and I can learn your deep, dark secrets," I teased.

"You are my deep, dark secret." He looked at me with the intensity that made me weak in the knees, then smiled like he was just teasing me.

"What else have you done?" I steered us away from his comment, even though I wanted more than anything to push him while he couldn't get away.

"Lots of things," he said dismissively, but I was looking at him expectantly, so he went on. "When I was young, Patrick got sick, so a physician came and made him better. I thought he was God and made it my goal to become a physician, so I could help people like he had. I worked long, hard hours as a laborer to afford medical school, and convinced our local physician to teach me everything he knew in the meantime. Then I died and lost every-thing, then we were raising Margaret... we were slightly overpro-tective, so she was my sole priority," he explained why having a child would prevent him from pursuing his career. "When she got married and didn't need me anymore..."

"That's when you went to war for the first time, right?" I asked because he was trying to explain that after Margaret died, he didn't see the point anymore, so he stopped caring and spent his time trying to die.

"The Seven Year's War," he agreed.

"Were you a medic?" He'd taught Terrence how to do that job during the Second World War.

"Not officially. The first time I enlisted, I didn't really care where they put me. When I inevitably died, I couldn't just go back to my unit as if nothing happened, so I kept finding new ones. If someone got injured, I used what I knew to help them. Some units made me their medic, but I wasn't recognized for it."

"Have you practiced since I met you? More than just stitching up friends?"

"I've always dabbled in it. Every few decades I go back to med school…"

"Is that necessary?" I cut him off. "Couldn't you just forge a new diploma, or edit the year on yours?"

"It was. When I started practicing, the United States didn't even have official medical schools. I went to Harvard when it opened and loved it. Graduated top of my class." He had a proud smile that made me smile too.

"A Harvard education wasn't good enough for you?" He basically lived my Ivy League dream. I was supposed to be at Harvard, enjoying my first year of pre-med. We had bigger concerns now, but a part of me needed to mourn the life I should have been living.

"It was incredible, but medicine is a field that is constantly improving and expanding. I usually wait a lifetime, then register as the son or the grandson of my previous self. Fraternities allow for legacies, so—"

"You were in a fraternity?" I raised my eyebrows. There were so many things I was learning about him, some of them completely unexpected.

"My roommate brought me in when I first attended, and it truly is a brotherhood that lasts forever. I use the fact that I'm a legacy to get recruited, but once initiation is over, there are higher levels of alumni who know about me. Some of them are Gifted too, which makes things a lot easier."

"Are there support groups for Gifted?" I imagined secret societies made up of people like him.

"More like friend groups," he considered it. "Embry established a group in Italy that he goes back to every few years. I have the fraternity whenever I go back to school, or who reach out sometimes for favors, but they're not exclusively like us. Sometimes we just run into people who wake up after dying, or who talk about the Great War like they were there… we make friends."

"Did you warn your friends I was coming to Harvard?" I realized what his fraternity ties implied.

"I was thrilled when you got in. Had things not gone… upside down, they would have invited you to join our sister sorority. I personally think you're better than that, but they feel it would be incredibly rude not to ask."

"I can't picture you as a preppy frat boy." I shook my head at the idea.

"I wasn't. I was in a fraternity, but I made sure I was a legacy, or there is no way I would get an invitation."

"Did Embry ever go to school with you? He's always had weird jobs whenever I ask."

"He's been a soldier, a barista, a few years of law school, but I don't think he finished."

"His painting is just a hobby, like your drawing?"

"How do you know about my drawing?" he asked.

"I always suspected it, but this was the proof." I showed him the moonstone necklace he gave me for my birthday, with an image of Sam, Deanna, and Clara that he scratched into the stone.

"I dabble," he dismissed his artistic side. "We both have properties and investments from so long ago that we don't need income, but we get bored sometimes. He likes to try new things, like ice cream shops and dog walking. I never know what he'll be doing." He smiled.

"What was your most recent job?"

"I've been working events more than jobs recently."

"Like concerts and festivals?" It didn't seem likely.

"No." He smiled at me and shook his head. "I got called in to work the Oklahoma City Bombing by an old FBI friend, then I volunteered as a doctor after 9/11…" he explained what he meant, and how he knew about the fertilizer bombs I made at the plantation.

"You help people," I summed it up.

"I try to," he agreed.

"What will you do when all of this is over?" For me, the likelihood was that it would never be over. I would either die because we lost, or because of the curse. For him, he had a deadline of ten years before he could do whatever he wanted for a few decades.

"Keep checking in on you, make sure you're okay and you get your happily ever after." He raised his shoulders like it was the same thing as always, but his eyes lingered on me before he looked out the window as we took off.

"What if everything goes right and we defeat him, and you guys get to live normal lives… don't you think you would want a break? To not worry about protecting someone else, but live your own life for a change?"

"I would definitely enjoy a stress-free vacation once we defeat Henry," he agreed, not really believing that was likely. "But no matter what happens, or where I am, you can always count on me. I will forever be there for you." We locked eyes and I could feel my cheeks burning before the seatbelt signs went off.

"Okay." I breathed, letting the moment linger a bit longer before looking at the screen in front of me. "Want to watch a movie?"

"Sure." He cleared his throat and adjusted his position before we settled in to watch an in-flight movie. It was a comedy that neither of us got into with all the other things on our minds, but it was nice to just sit there and pretend we weren't on our way to find things to help break a curse that would kill me if we didn't reverse it, and stop the Big Bad who wanted to rip my heart out.

CHAPTER TWELVE

"That was so much smoother. No offence," I told Gabriel once the plane taxied into its spot and the seatbelt sign went off. I'm sure he was an excellent pilot, and it wasn't like we crashed, but the crop duster he flew us to Terrence's in was near the bottom of my favorite modes of transportation list. Barely a step above boats.

"It's a very different plane," he pointed out.

"My first real plane ride." I smiled despite the terrible circumstances. "Again, no offence."

"None taken," he assured me, grabbing his bag of weapons so we could make our way through the crowded airport.

Embry joined us not long after, with one of the flight attendants smiling at him. It wasn't a flirtatious smile, more like she was grateful.

"I take it you had a pleasant flight?"

"She's going through a very hard time. She's flying all over the place while her son lives with her parents and she's trying to pay her way through school so she can support him, and... it was an interesting flight." He stopped himself from sharing her entire life story, but I understood that he made her feel better, if only for a while.

"What do we do now?" I asked once we were outside. There was a line of taxis waiting to bring passengers to hotels, buses to tourist destinations, rental car services... "Do we just go to his place and ring the doorbell?"

"I had an old friend look into it. As far as the government is concerned, the property is owned by a Ric Dawson, who's been there since 2000," Embry shared.

"Does that mean we don't know how to find him?"

"It would. Only Ric inherited it from a great uncle, so he might just be a Gifted who is on top of his paperwork."

EMBRY USED a fake driver's license to rent us a black sedan, so Gabriel used the map they gave us to locate Dawes Estate. I knew I was naïve and too trusting, but I really didn't get the impression that the man from Cassie's memory would ever want to hurt me.

It was a three-hour drive before we stopped at a bed-and-breakfast. It was charming and rustic, giving the impression that there was no internet and probably not even cable, but it was welcoming and felt safe. Not to say that I trusted it, but it was a lot better than the motel.

Embry used his fake name and got us two adjoining rooms, which he paid for in cash.

"How far are we from the estate?" I asked Gabriel while Embry had a conversation with the woman who owned the B and B about the history of the area.

"Five or ten minutes. There are a couple more houses, then it's the property, but he has as much land as you do."

"What's your feeling about him?" I asked.

"I haven't met him yet."

"But we're here, in England, for no other reason than—"

"Than to get things from your ancestors so we can save you. If he can help us, great, but I won't be trusting him."

WE WALKED UP to the front door with the two of them standing in front of me, forming a wall in case he wasn't friendly. His manor was a lot like ours, in the sense that it seemed cold from the outside, but I heard laughter when we got close, and wondered if it was just as warm as my home used to be.

"How can I help you?" A woman in her thirties opened the door, covered in glitter, still smiling from whatever adventures we interrupted.

"We were looking for—"

"Ric!" As soon as she spotted me, she called into the room on her left, where all the laughter was coming from.

Embry and Gabriel both put their arms out to hold me back. I could feel the tension in their bodies. Friend or foe, we were in the right place.

"What is it?" Ric asked. A little blonde girl giggled over his shoulder while another was wrapped around his leg. It was him, but there were wisps of gray in his hair that hadn't been there in the memory. He smiled at the guys before his eyes landed on me. I tensed up, knowing he would react, but I relaxed when he looked at me like I looked at Gabriel when he showed up in the field behind the gas station after I thought he died. "You're not Judith, or Cassie." Ric gave me a sad smile.

"Lucy," I agreed.

"Come on in." He handed the smaller of the girls to the woman and lifted the one from his leg up into his arms.

Gabriel and Embry exchanged a look before following him into the house.

The inside looked like a real estate agent staged it, then a mini tornado ran through it. The decor was elegant and beautiful, but there were books, pictures, teddies, and things that turned houses into homes strewn all over. Not that it was messy, just… lived in.

"You are Alaric Dawes, right?" I asked once we got to the kitchen. He motioned for us to sit, then put a kettle on the stove.

"Older than you expected?" He asked me, still smiling. The constant happiness would worry me, but I didn't have to be Embry to know it was genuine.

"You've done pretty well since I saw in you in 1840, but I was under the impression you wouldn't age."

"I didn't. Until one day I did." He looked over to the woman, probably his wife, and they exchanged a smile that reminded me of Sam and Deanna.

"What were you supposed to do?" I asked.

"All I thought I had was money, so I've spent many lives running charities, doing aid trips to Africa, sponsoring children and rainforests and doing everything I could imagine that would be helpful to the world. I long ago resigned myself to living forever alone, but then I met Sarah." He smiled over at her. "I had no intentions of falling in love, so I kept my distance until one night, I selfishly accept her offer for pizza and a play at the Globe with some friends who worked with us. By the end of the night, I knew I was done for, but I had no idea how to tell her. Not even five minutes after I left her house, I came across a mugging. A pregnant woman. The guy had a gun, she was terrified, he looked like he might use it… I couldn't die anyway, so I stopped it and then, suddenly, I had grey hairs," he shared.

"Who was she?" I asked, noting that both my guys were apprehensive, not at all ready to trust this man spilling his guts in front of us.

"I don't know, but some day, either she or her son will do something hopefully wonderful, and I just had to be in that place at that time."

"When you say you just got grey hairs…" I let it linger, hoping he would elaborate on the process. "I've never met anyone who was Gifted and isn't anymore," I admitted.

"I don't think it's the same for everyone, but I was given a choice. The light was there, and I knew I could walk into it and be reunited with everyone I loved... but Sarah was a few blocks away, and the way my heart skipped a beat at the thought of her, I knew I had to see where it went," he explained. "You call us Gifted?"

"You don't?" I turned it on him.

"Jude always called people like me Supernaturals." He shrugged.

"Jude being Judith?"

"She was brilliant, in every sense of the word," he agreed before the kettle sang. "Tea?"

"Thank you."

The guys declined, so he poured milk into three mugs, added tea, then handed one to me, one to Sarah, and kept the last for himself.

"I'm here because I need to find something of hers. I don't know how well you knew her, but I was hoping you could help." It wasn't exactly true. I knew from Cassie's memory that he knew her very well, but I wasn't going to tell him that.

"Why do you need something of hers?"

"It's a long story," I dismissed his question.

"Forgive me if I see you and talk like you're her. I imagine saying you can trust me won't mean much?"

"Not really," I apologized.

"How did you know her?" Gabriel asked.

"She was my wife."

I could tell that the guys were just as shocked as I was.

"Does that make you..."

"Your ancestor," he agreed. "Jude was my best friend and my first love. I was ready to marry her the day I met her, this beautiful and insanely smart woman who didn't take no for an answer... but she had no intentions of settling down until she conquered the world. I waited through school, her crush on a prick from her class, even her running away to study under a private tutor in Spain. She wrote, but I didn't know if being her friend was worse than being nothing, so I never responded. When she came home, she was furious, and after telling me so, she proposed to me."

"Very progressive," I commented.

"She knew what she wanted and usually went after it," he explained. "It was only a few months after we got married that I died on a hunting trip with my brother. I was just as shocked as my nephew who shot me a second time, this one on purpose. Jude came immediately, did hours of research, sat by my side while my brother, a physician, ran test after test without figuring out what was wrong with me. I told her to leave me, that she deserved a husband, not an abomination, but she told me she just wanted someone who would love her and our child, and really hoped that person would be me." He was beaming. "They were born a few months later, and we lived happily ever after for a few years, until we lost her."

"When you say 'they' were born?" It was Embry who asked. I also wondered if there was a whole other branch to my family tree, another me out there that needed protecting.

"We had twins. Josephine and Oliver, after my father," he shared.

"Did they take your last name?" All my ancestors after Annabelle kept Owens.

"They did," he agreed. "We lost Oliver to measles when the twins were eight. Josephine never quite got over it, but she insisted on doing all the things he made her promise she would do. We had many adventures before I had to let her go."

"You didn't keep track of them?" Gabriel asked, with a slight accusation.

"I did, until Esther told me they were moving to the colonies. I wanted to come with her, but my little Esther said it was her adventure and promised she would write. Which she did, but her daughter, Annabelle, didn't know me enough to carry on the tradition." The guys perked up at the mention of Annabelle.

"How old was Judith when she died?" I asked, trying to be delicate, but I was pretty sure I knew the answer.

"Almost twenty-nine," he shared. "Cancer."

"I'm so sorry," I told him.

"Thank you," he said, though the words were meaningless. "Why do you ask?"

"All of us who look like her... we've all been dying at the same age. That's why I need something of hers."

"For a spell?" He asked.

"Judith was a witch?"

"Sometimes. She had an unpleasant experience before we got together, so she mostly stayed away from it, but the twins got sick when they were barely a year old, and she did some kind of protection spell that required something belonging to each of them."

"This is like that," I agreed.

"I have her portrait in the attic, which would be how my wife recognized you," he answered a question I was definitely going to get to. "But as far as something that belonged to her..." He brought his hand to his chin, trying to think of something. "I gave her ring to John when he proposed to Josephine, who got all her jewelry... I have a box in the attic, but it's mostly papers... I'll go get it." He went off, leaving the three of us with his wife.

"You're taking this really well," I said to her after a minute of sitting there awkwardly.

"It was difficult to believe that he used to wake up every time he died and was alive when my great-great-grandparents were born, but he's worth it," she told me. "I asked about the painting when he showed me the attic. He explained that she was his wife, who died, told me how he ran into one of their descendants who was the spitting image of her and nearly had a heart attack."

"At least you were prepared."

"Oh, nothing surprises me now," she assured me.

ALARIC CAME DOWN with a round hat box that held their marriage license, partially disintegrated letters, and an old pair of glasses.

"Were these hers?" I asked hopefully.

"Oliver's," he said sadly, picking them up. "But this was hers." He found a handkerchief underneath them. "Her something blue." He smiled.

"Do you mind if I take it?" I asked. "I don't know if you'll be able to get it back after I'm done with it," I warned.

"A decade ago, I might have held on, but I'm good now." He looked over to Sarah.

"Thank you. You have no idea what this means."

"It means someone else won't have to lose you like I lost her," he let me know he understood.

"Daddy, we're hungry." One of the girls came in and tugged on Alaric's sleeve.

"Is that so?" he asked her.

"Yes, and it's nearly supper time, and Poppy was thinking we could maybe have chicken nuggets."

"Poppy thought that?" he questioned her.

"Yes," the girl lied, but she was committed.

"Would you like to stay for supper?" Sarah offered.

"We wouldn't want to impose," I argued.

"It would be our pleasure," she told me. "We don't entertain nearly enough, and Ric always makes industrious quantities of chicken nuggets."

"We can stay," Embry assured me.

· · ·

"DID YOU KNOW JUDITH'S PARENTS?" I asked Alaric once he put the nuggets in the oven. Sarah was making a salad, and the guys were talking in hushed voices.

"I did." There was a question to his answer, like when I'd asked about surnames.

"We thought Annabelle was the earliest one who looked like me. I'm wondering if there was another one before Judith."

"When I met Cassandra, she wondered the same thing," he admitted.

"Did she find out?"

"She left before we could do any research, but I tried to look into it for her."

"What did you discover?"

"This was centuries ago, so I was working with a very limited paper trail, but I found a few generations at the County Records Office in town."

"That's really helpful. I'll check it out in the morning," I told him.

"Do you already have a place to stay?"

"We do, but thank you for the offer."

"You're always welcome here," he assured me.

THE NUGGETS WERE DELICIOUS. Alaric's daughters, Poppy and Violet, were hilarious and adorable with their British accents. I could tell the guys were uncomfortable and only said we could stay to let me find out more about Judith's ancestry, so I declined Sarah's offer of cake.

"Thank you so much for everything," I told Alaric, giving him a hug. It was nice to find out about a decent male ancestor of mine for a change.

"It was my pleasure." He smiled. I believed he meant it, even though I brought up so many sad moments of his life. "And Lucy, I hope you succeed," he told me.

"Me too," I agreed.

GABRIEL DROVE us back to the bed-and-breakfast, with neither of us talking much.

"How many do you think we have left?" Embry wondered as we climbed the stairs.

"I don't know, but we'll have to make sure before we attempt the spell. It said all of them, and I don't want to see what happens if we only have some." Gabriel was concerned.

"Ric says there were records at the County Records Office. We could go there and trace back from Judith, like researching a family tree," I suggested.

"Keep going back until we can't go back any further." Embry sighed.

"I also have the dreams… hopefully they can help steer us in the right direction."

"We'll head out first thing in the morning," Gabriel decided.

"After breakfast?" I tried. "The brochure says that her clotted cream is the best in the country."

"We can grab a quick bite." Embry smiled and ruffled my hair before we went to the rooms. The guys were sharing one with two double beds, while I got the king to myself. I closed the adjoining door while I changed and got ready for bed, but left it open for the night, in case anything happened.

It was weird, because everything was still scary, and I was hunting down an unknown number of needles in a field of haystacks, but Sam being alive and finding Judith's handkerchief made me feel like somehow, I might get through this.

CHAPTER THIRTEEN

The following morning, we drove into town to get a look at the records. The three of us walked into the building together, but Gabriel and I stayed back while Embry used his Gift to make the woman behind the desk trust him.

"They're public records. You can't take the books out, but anyone can access them," she assured him.

"Thank you."

He nodded for us to follow him to the second story of the building, which was set up like a very small library, only all the books were basically ledgers and registries.

"Is there an index?" Gabriel asked, but I was already going through the cards by the desk. It was empty, and by the looks of it, no one ever worked there. It was more for people consulting the books.

I found Judith and Ric's marriage license, then used that to track down her birth certificate. "They hold death, marriage, and birth certificates in the blue books. Now that I know Judith was born in 1540 to George and Irene, I can look up when her parents were born and find their parents and so on," I explained what I was doing.

"I'll look into her father." Embry went to get the right year for him, while Gabriel went to get her mother's, and I scribbled down everything about Judith that might eventually be useful.

"I THINK I'VE FOUND ONE," I ventured, stumbling upon an ancestor with a mother named Kiara. "You needed parental consent to marry before twenty-one, but her mother was deceased." I showed them the marriage certificate.

"Kiara?" Embry asked. Thanks to 'Kiara's Cure', the name itself was enough to tell me we had to look into it.

"According to Saoirse's birth certificate, she was born in Ireland." I handed it over.

"Meaning we have to find the building like this in Ireland to go any further?" Gabriel verified.

"We also have the place Saoirse was born. If it was a family home they had for generations…" I let the thought linger, not sure what I was hoping to find other than memories. Unless a relative of mine was still living there, it was very unlikely that I would find any kind of paperwork in a house that old.

"Haven't they digitized all of this yet?" Embry asked, putting the books we were no longer using back on their shelves.

"Not anywhere that I can find without raising suspicions," I turned him down. I wanted to google all this recent information to find out more, but if my enemies were using computer chips to track us, I was not going to chance it.

"What's on your mind?" Gabriel asked when I stared at the word 'deceased'.

"Do you think Henry had anything to do with it, or did he only start hunting us after Annabelle?" I asked. "Do either of you know how old he is?"

"Older than us, but I don't know more than that," Gabriel told me.

"I wonder if he knew all of them." I thought back to my memories of him. "He didn't look like he knew Annabelle when he saved her, but he might have spotted her from a distance and approached her because he knew she was one of the Bearers. But he seemed genuinely surprised when she could do magic."

"You can check his memories after we kill him." Gabriel didn't like my intimate knowledge of him. He worried that the more I knew about Henry, the harder it would be for me to harm him, or allow them to. He underestimated how much I despised the man.

"I'll find us a boat." Embry sighed.

"A real one, or—"

"They have ferries to Ireland, I'll do my best," he told me before we followed him outside.

We already had all our possessions, so we drove the rental car back to one of the company's locations and made our way to the ferry on foot. Embry took us through a shortcut to avoid the larger crowds.

"Have you lived in England before?" I asked him. He'd barely used a map since we landed.

"Not exactly. I've visited many times, stayed for long stretches, but never long enough to buy a place to call my own."

"And you stayed with…" I let it linger. I knew they were both in love with Annabelle and utterly devoted to her, at least until Embry met Beth, but I couldn't imagine that they never even entertained the thought of other women for those three centuries.

"Other Gifted, mostly."

"Delia is from here, originally," Gabriel shared. "Still has family in the area, but I can't risk contacting her. Or them."

"Are they okay?" I asked. I last saw Delia when she, Tristan, and Benjamin travelled to Florida to be decoys for me, Gabriel, and Embry. She had told Gabriel she missed him, but I didn't think there was anything there. Or maybe I didn't want there to be.

"They left word that they made it safely. I haven't heard them ask for help, but such a request wouldn't come to us. It would have gone to someone else in the network who was closer, and not busy protecting you."

"Is she who you stayed with?" I asked Embry.

Before he had the chance to answer, a man with long black hair and an eyebrow ring walked over from the street and stopped right in front of me. My breath caught in my chest as I brought my hands up, waiting to see his eyes, or for him to make a move to tell me if he was just a weird tourist, or someone trying to kill me.

"You came," he said, as five other people arrived and stood around us. I had yet to master 360° freezing, so I couldn't take care of everyone at once, but I also wanted to know what he was talking about.

"How did you find us?" I asked the man who, for the moment, seemed more intent on scaring me than killing me.

"We've been waiting for you."

"In this alley?" I looked around to see if there was something special about it, but came up short.

"Don't play innocent," he warned. "You won't get it."

"Get what?" I asked, but he had already pulled out his weapon, as did all his friends. I couldn't freeze them all, but I wasn't prepared to blow them into smithereens either.

I put up my shield when he came at me and sent him flying back into some garbage bins. The guys each took on two of the assailants, meaning I didn't have a clear shot until they stood still. I grabbed a discarded piece of wood from the pile of trash nearest me and hit one of the men attacking Embry. I thought I got him on the head and incapacitated him, at least a little, but he turned around and faced me with nothing but anger and annoyance.

He charged at me, sending some kind of blue light ahead of him, so I quickly put up my force shield. He bounced back, but not nearly as far as people usually did. This angered him further, but Gabriel was down to one attacker, so he stabbed him in the stomach with the dagger and came to my defense. His speed was the only thing that put him on somewhat of an equal footing with the man, who had the build of a lumberjack and seemed unfazed by most of our attacks. When I got a clear shot, I froze him, which allowed Gabriel to knock him out for good.

"Follow me." Embry called out once our attackers were on the ground, though I wasn't naïve enough to believe they would stay there. We ran through a couple of alleys, to the busier streets, and didn't stop until we got to the docks.

"We'll take three tickets to Ireland," Embry told the woman, charming her with his Gift while we tried to look normal.

"They're boarding in a few minutes." She gave him a smile as she handed over our tickets.

"What were they doing there?" I asked, looking worriedly back to the city, but no one was following us as we headed for the line at the end of the dock.

"How would he know we would be here? Judith lived hours from here, and those men weren't following us. They were waiting." Gabriel was upset, but I appreciated him thinking out loud instead of in hushed voices with Embry once I was no longer around.

"Do you think they have another tracker on us?"

"No, I think there is something here that Henry expects us to be after," Embry argued.

"Where exactly were we when they found us?" I asked.

"A tiny alley."

"I know that, but was there anything nearby? A museum with relics from Crescent Moon Bearers, a magic shop with grimoires… he told me there was a spell, but I don't think he would know we've already found it." I was thinking out loud.

"We can't assume he doesn't know everything we do. We need

to act like he has spies following us every step of the way," Gabriel argued.

"There was an old bookshop, but I don't think it has any occult origins. There were business buildings close by, a church, shopping—"

"A church might make sense. You said Henry's people couldn't go into churches, which could explain why they were waiting outside in the alley," I suggested.

"It's an old church, I don't think they have a museum or anything. It's not a tourist attraction," Embry argued.

"What's it called?"

"Sacred Heart."

We got to the end of the line and stood behind a girl who looked to be about fourteen, travelling with an older woman in a wheelchair, doing patchwork by the looks of it.

"Excuse me, is that a pamphlet for Sacred Heart?" I asked, noticing the paper in her hand. It was like a newsletter, only it had the name of the church and an enormous picture of a cross on the front of it.

"It's just the weekly church newsletter. It's hers," she told me before bending down closer to the older woman, who reacted when she heard the name of the church. She said something to her in a language I didn't understand, before turning to me, "She says they have mass at seven every evening, but you won't make it back in time if you take the ferry," she dismissed the older woman.

"Is it worth checking out on our way back?"

"She says their old priest now lives in Rome, and he brought the Lignum Crucis this week to celebrate the church's anniversary or something," the girl translated.

"What's the Lignum Crucis?" I asked her.

"The true cross," she told me. "Any authentic fragments of the cross Christ was crucified on are known as Lignum cruces."

"Thank you so much." I smiled at the teenager, who took out

headphones and put them on before I could ask her any more questions.

"That's Emmanuel's Betrayal." I turned to the guys and whispered, using the spell's term for the Cross Jesus was crucified on. "That has to be it."

"Why would Henry think we were going after the ingredients to his ritual?" Embry asked.

"He already said he has all the ingredients except for you, so it's not like we can collect them first and stop him," Gabriel pointed out.

"And the coalescence is a ritual only he can do, right?" I looked from one to the other, but they both shrugged.

"Not necessarily. We are here to protect you, but that doesn't mean that someone else can't stand in the way of you getting hurt. Your destiny is shaped by many things," Gabriel explained.

"You're saying we can complete the ritual instead of him?" I confirmed, momentarily disregarding the fact that it involved ripping out my heart.

"I don't know enough about the ritual to answer you as far as magic goes, but I know that even if he is staying alive to complete it, that doesn't mean that someone else couldn't."

"But Henry definitely thinks we're going after the ritual's ingredients."

"Which means we could stay under the radar by not going after them." Embry saw what I was hinting at.

"But if we're supposed to be getting them, shouldn't we?"

"Do you think it can help us?" Gabriel wasn't so quick to turn me down, but he didn't look convinced either.

"Even before I knew magic was real, I knew that you can't bring people back to life. If Annabelle and Beth had the spell but never used it, I'm thinking it can't be so easy as putting some things in a bowl and saying a few words."

"You think only someone who has completed the ritual can use the spell?" Gabriel turned to Embry to see what he thought of it.

"That would explain why he thinks we're going after it. The ritual ingredients were in public books, and lots of people tried to complete it. But Kiara's cure, based on the name, was probably tailor-made for my family."

"Is this something you want to do?" Embry asked me, resigning himself to it.

"I don't want to, but I would much rather have one of you cut my heart out and have undying power than Henry."

"Then it's settled. We're getting all the ingredients." He sighed, neither of them happy about it.

CHAPTER FOURTEEN

"It's so beautiful," I said, mostly to myself, but Gabriel was beside me, so he took a break from watching the other passengers to take in the scenery. The ferry to Ireland was better than a boat, but I still preferred land travel. We were nearing our third hour, and I was ready to get off.

"It's green," was his response.

"It's luscious green. I have never wanted to run through a field and roll around in the grass, but I want to do that now."

He looked at me like he was suddenly struck by how young and immature I was.

"Nothing excites you anymore?" I turned to face him instead of the view.

"I guess I'm letting the context get in the way. You look at it as a silver lining to this trip, but I'm seeing all the places people could hide, marred by memories…"

"What memories?"

"I have happy ones, like spending weeks with Terrence's family when I was best man at his wedding, but there have been wars, famines, escaping dangerous people…."

"With Cassie?"

"Sometimes I help other people too," he admitted.

"With the FBI?" I whispered, but more to tease him than to keep it a secret.

"There are amazing people in the world who see someone in need and go out of their way to help them. There are other people who see a weakness and exploit it. Who see something they want and take it, whether it belongs to them or not. When those people have Gifts, they believe the normal rules don't apply to them. We have the safe houses for those types of situations, but sometimes it's safest to be constantly moving."

"We have time, if you wanted to give me an example of these people," I pointed out. It would be at least another hour until we arrived in Ireland.

"Maybe forty years ago, there was a Gifted who decided his task was to liberate all the child soldiers of the world. It was a beautiful dream, and his Gift was that he could open anything, so he could easily free them once he found them. He got some hired guns for protection, but it cost a lot of lives, both from him and from the children he tried to rescue. He recuperated at the safe house a few times when a friend of Caleb's was the guardian, and the conversation turned to Etta and her Gift. The guy saw this as his solution to save all kids, but instead of bringing the injured to her, or asking if she could help, he kidnapped her, chained her to the back of a van, and forced her to fix people for him."

"That's… he was trying to do a good thing in a terrible way," I tried to translate my thoughts into words.

"Our callings can drive us mad. Especially if you don't have an end in sight. Was it one particular child he had to save, or did he have to keep saving them until there were no more child soldiers? I'm sure he started out with the best of intentions, but he eventually built his own army of unwilling soldiers."

"Did you just rescue her, or did you take care of him too? Are there prisons for Gifted?" I asked, so many questions floating around my mind.

"There is one prison that has a section to contain Gifted. There are rooms and devices that can contain Gifts, but before that they would cater cells to the Gifted. When I was a government man, there was a block of cells we visited, where the guards wore hazmat suits tailored to each Gift. As long as they couldn't touch you, you couldn't hear them, and they couldn't make eye contact, you were safe."

"That seems like..."

"A lot of trouble. There are Gifted who, although they're not bad people, don't like being locked up, or held accountable for the things they do. A lot of them will hang themselves to get out, but if you stumble upon someone who knows what you are... it's not like we did that for every Gifted who got arrested, but if the crime was violent, we kept them contained."

"Which prison?" I asked. "Guantanamo, Alcatraz..."

"Rikers," he shared. "But don't tell anyone I told you, because it is way above your clearance level."

"My lips are sealed," I assured him with a smile.

I convinced him to tell me more about his times in Ireland, finally getting him to admit that the Emerald Isle could be beautiful if you weren't on the run or fighting for your life, before Embry came back with food.

"What did I miss?" He asked, handing me a chicken and pesto panini.

"I'd say we're about an hour out, but I can see it and it's gorgeous," I filled him in.

"Half an hour according to the screens inside, but I'm glad you're enjoying this boat ride." He smiled.

"Enjoying is a stretch, but it's the best I've had yet."

"At least you've got delightful company?" Embry tried.

"And time to go over the Chronicles, the Book of Shadows, and everything we know about Henry's ritual."

"Did you come to any conclusions?" Gabriel asked me.

"We know of six ingredients needed to complete it. The

kindling from Emmanuel's Betrayal is what those men were trying to stop us from getting. They can't possibly be watching every single piece of the cross, because there are thousands. But then again, none of them can prove their authenticity. The church recognizes some as more likely, but that's it."

"Our best bet would be to collect all of them and hope at least one of them is real," Gabriel said like it was a plan rather than an impossible setback.

"The soul of his untouched child just means a virgin, which sounds sketchy, but since my life is at stake either way, I might as well risk my soul." I swallowed, aware that my face was burning red at that admission. "Tears of Isis are the easiest, because you can buy vervain pretty much everywhere."

"The arms of Yggdrasil?" Embry pressed.

"That's where it gets complicated. Yggdrasil is an imaginary tree that connects the Nine Worlds in Norse mythology."

"What does that mean?" Gabriel furrowed his brow.

"It means I have no idea where we can find it because it's a mythical thing and no one knows where it is."

"Henry said he had everything except for your heart," Embry pointed out. It couldn't be imaginary.

"We'll figure it out," Gabriel assured me.

I wanted to argue with his optimism, but I could tell it was determination and he would get it done. "The blood of the incumbent means whoever does it has to prick themselves." I moved on to the next ingredient. "And we all know about my heart," I finished.

"Which he will never get," Embry vowed.

"Fingers crossed," I agreed, getting him to roll his eyes at me. "I've also been trying to figure out how Beth got Kiara's Cure. I think she and Cassie knew more than they let on." I bit my bottom lip and looked to Embry for his reaction.

"We didn't keep any secrets." He gave me an intense stare that could rival Gabriel's, then sighed. "But she liked to research and look into things on her own. She might have found something she was waiting to get more information on before sharing with me."

I gave him a smile before looking back out at the expanse of our destination. He seemed convinced, but there had to be a reason no one ever mentioned a spell that could save us to the men responsible for protecting us. Maybe we were right, and it didn't work unless you completed the ritual first. Perhaps it came with terrible consequences that they weren't prepared to pay. Either way, I hoped Ireland held the answers we were looking for. But I had a bad feeling about what we would find.

CHAPTER FIFTEEN

When we finally docked in Ireland, I was more than happy to set foot on solid ground, even if I still felt wobbly. We used a tourist map to find the address Saoirse was born at in 1462, not expecting to find much, since we knew she ended up in England, but I was hoping for more than a literal pile of rubble.

"The parish church should have some records." Embry put his hand on my shoulder.

"Maybe they'll have a family plot in the cemetery." I was staying optimistic, but I was no genealogist, and the farther back we went, the harder it would be to track my ancestors down. Not to mention we had no way of knowing when the first one of us appeared.

It was a short walk to the parish cathedral made of large stones. I took the 'est. 1225' as a good sign for finding information on Kiara, but we wouldn't be able to go much further than that.

"Good morning," a priest walked over and whispered as soon as we opened the doors. "Are you here for the mass?"

"No, we're..." I looked back to the guys, but it was a small building, and everyone looked busy at the moment. "Yes, we are," I decided.

"Wonderful, it's just starting." He ushered us over to some pews near the back. I made sure to kneel and do the sign of the cross before taking my seat.

I hadn't been in church for ages. Mrs. Boyd used to bring me with her, but after she died, Mr. Boyd didn't see the point in it. *'God is everywhere. Why should I have to go to church to talk to him?'* was his answer the one time I asked about it.

I only said yes to put us in the priest's good graces and not disturb the mass, but being back in a church brought me so many questions. I always believed in God and Jesus in a very compartmental way. When they taught us about the Big Bang in school, I listened and accepted it as fact. But I also knew that God created the earth and people and everything I read in the Bible. Both facts existed in my brain simultaneously, as long as I never tried to figure out which was right.

I spent most of the service trying to decide what I believed in, given my new knowledge of Magic and Gifted, and the upheaval of everything I took for granted. By the end, I determined I would need a third compartment to make sense of it all and allow magic, religion, and science to co-exist in my mind.

We followed the dozen or so congregation members towards the exit, but the priest who let us in stopped us before we could talk to the priest who said mass.

"Are you interested in a tour as well?" he asked us. He was a plain man in his forties, but he had a smile that made his eyes twinkle.

"That would be lovely," I said, speaking for the group again.

"I'm Father Dunn." He extended his hand to shake mine, then did the same for Gabriel and Embry. "What brings you to Killaloe?"

"I've been working on my family tree, and one of my ancestors was born a few minutes from here back in 1462," I gave him a partial answer.

"That's exciting!" His enthusiasm seemed genuine, but misplaced for someone his age, in his profession. "I grew up not even ten minutes from here. What's the name?"

"Saoirse Muldoon," I shared, reading his face for any sign of recollection. The guys were staying close, but so far letting me handle it.

"Don't know any Muldoons in town, but we have records going back to the late fifteenth century, if you want to know more about it," he offered.

"That would be brilliant, thank you."

He brought us to a small office in the back and went through stacks of black volumes before he found the one he was looking for. "We've been digitizing the records to make them more comprehensible. Faded ink and elegant handwriting are not helpful when trying to decipher names and dates," he shared.

"This is incredible, thank you." I flipped through the printed pages representing church records of the time.

"You can't search by people, but if you know when in 1462, you can find the entry that records her birth."

"January 1st." I found her faster than I would have expected. "If her mother was born here, would she also be in the book?"

"This is the oldest book we have. It goes all the way back to 1425. We lost anything before then in a fire."

"Deaths too?" Embry inquired.

"Anything a priest would have presided over," he agreed. "Can I fetch you all some tea?"

"Thank you," Gabriel told him.

It surprised me that he left us alone in the office, but it seemed to be a pretty small town.

"You're going to go through every page?" Embry asked me.

"We know she died before 1480, so it's just eighteen years," I said, flipping through the pages to find it. "Kiara Muldoon died in 1468," I showed them. "They found it shocking, probably because she was only twenty-eight."

"Can you remember anything?" Gabriel tried.

"Maybe if I touched her tombstone, or we can go back to the pile of rocks later?"

"Let's see how far back we can go, then we'll ask Father Dunn about her grave," Embry suggested.

I KEPT SEARCHING after Father Dunn came back with the teas, scribbling names and dates onto a post-it while Embry and he discussed World War One. I wouldn't have pegged him as such a war aficionado, but Embry recognized a medal on the desk and the conversation flowed.

"Did you find what you were looking for?" Father Dunn asked when I eventually closed the volume. Kiara was either first generation, or her parents were born before the fire.

"This was really helpful," I agreed. "Do you think you could point us to where she was buried?"

"Let me see." He came over to see her death entry, that I'd bookmarked, but got uncomfortable as he read the information. "She's not in our plot," he told me delicately.

"What do you mean?" I asked, going back to the book. I saw nothing wrong with her entry, other than a few symbols underneath her name, but every death notice had a variety of symbols.

"This symbol here means she'll be in the Cillin." he waited for me to understand, but I didn't.

"What's a Cillin?"

"It's a special burial place for stillborn babies, and the ones that die before we can baptize them," Gabriel filled me in, but he directed it to the priest, since Kiara was neither.

"It's for anyone who didn't have the right to a proper catholic burial."

"As in she wasn't catholic?" I pressed.

"It says she died of suicide."

"She killed herself?" I was shocked, and by the looks of it, so were Embry and Gabriel.

"I'm sorry," Father Dunn apologized. "The closest one isn't that far, but they're unmarked graves."

"Might be worth a look." I tried to smile in gratitude. It wasn't that she killed herself that bothered me; it was the thought that maybe she did it because the bad guys were closing in, and they buried her as a sinner after she sacrificed herself to save the world.

"Here, I'll write down the directions for you, and if there's anything else I can help you with, just let me know." He handed me another post-it, so we thanked him for the teas and headed out.

WE LEFT by the back of the church to follow the Father's directions and encountered a colossal statue of the Virgin Mary in the courtyard.

"Henry definitely had something to do with it." I bit my bottom lip and looked up at them. I still wasn't sure I believed that he was evil from the start of his relationship with Annabelle, but I couldn't face the idea that Kiara just gave up. Especially when they named the Cure after her.

"Or someone like him," Gabriel agreed, which surprised me. He was the last person I expected to hear defending Henry, of all people.

"That's probably why they moved to England."

"It would have been quite the scandal," Embry agreed.

I absent-mindedly ran my fingers along the bottom of the statue, but as soon as my hand touched the smooth rock, everything went blurry...

FROM WHAT I COULD TELL, I looked exactly like myself, and all the other Bearers, but I was someone new. I'd been through it with Beth, but it was still a shock to feel the baby kick my bladder. The woman whose memory I was in, probably Kiara, didn't even notice the kick. She was staring up at the Virgin Mary statue, with tears pouring down her face and a war between guilt and determination in her heart.

She left the statue and scurried through the streets, looking over her shoulder like she was being followed and expected an attack at any moment. She turned down a street where it seemed like the sun vanished. As if the clouds of smoke from the chimneys all converged together to block out any light. I shivered and, though Kiara stood tall and kept walking, she also pulled her shawl tighter around herself.

When she got to a rather large wooden shack with dead animals hanging beside the doorway, she paused and took a deep breath. She brought her hand to her bulging stomach and rubbed it protectively, taking more deep breaths to stop the tears that had been falling ever since this memory started. One more and she knocked.

"I was hoping you wouldn't come," the woman said as a greeting. She left the door open, but that was the only welcome Kiara got as the woman went back to chopping something putrid-smelling and purple.

"If there were any other option, I wouldn't have." Kiara looked right into the woman's eyes, her jaw set.

"This is dark magic, love. Not the kind you can take back." The old woman softened, but still looked disappointed. Her hair was just as curly as mine, but much longer and blonde. Her face had many wrinkles, but I would have bet money she got them from smiling more than frowning. Except today.

"I know."

"Are you sure about this Kiara? Curses come with consequences that no one can predict. Putting a curse on yourself doubles the danger."

"Saoirse is far away and safe with her father, but if they get me, it

won't matter where they are or what we do. The power they would gain is unimaginable. They would be unstoppable, wreaking havoc on the world, immune to any manmade weapons, resistant to most magic... if one life can save millions, how can I not?"

"But it isn't just one life, is it?" The woman eyed Kiara's stomach, which she cradled protectively.

"They're still a few days out and he's nearly ready."

"You'll wait?" For the first time, the woman was hopeful.

"I will do everything in my power to keep him safe." My voice shook as the tears slowly rolled down my cheeks. But Kiara's determination did not waver.

"God help you." The woman shook her head before grabbing two pieces of paper from a small wooden chest, and a handful of powders.

"You couldn't have called it Kiara's Brave Sacrifice?" Kiara asked after reading the title of the first paper, as the woman crushed the powders together. Kiara's Curse sounded intriguing until you realized it was Kiara's Curse on Kiara.

"I call it as I see it, not as you wish it to be."

"And this reverses it?" she asked of the second sheet.

"It ends the Curse. As long as you haven't done the unspeakable, it will be like this never happened."

"It won't be in my lifetime," Kiara said to herself, reading the Cure I'd already seen in the Chronicles. "Is all of this necessary?"

"It's a simple list of items you have in your chest at home." The woman sounded exasperated with Kiara's being difficult, but Kiara knew she wouldn't be the one using the Cure. It was nice of her to realize that her descendants wouldn't find the list as easy to track down, but she might have considered preparing us for it.

"Is it ready?" The powders she had been mixing were producing a yellow cloud of smoke that moved like it was alive, unmolested by the wind, smelling out its environment.

"Give me your hand." The old woman sighed. I would have thought she was annoyed, or bored, but there was something in her eyes that made me think she cared so much that this was the only way she could *get through what she was about to do. As soon as I gave her my left hand, she sliced it open with a tiny blue blade. The drops of my blood sizzled once they touched the powder, turning the smoke to a rust-like color.*

"A warning would have been nice," I said, but the woman put her finger on top of the wound and used my blood to paint a crescent moon on her forehead.

"If I give myself the chance, I will change my mind," she explained her abrupt manner. "Have you memorized it?"

"I have."

"Then take my hand, sister, and let ye be damned." Her steely gaze broke as her glassy eyes watered. We held hands and started chanting in a language I didn't understand. The Curse was long, but they repeated it over and over, so it no longer sounded like words, but like a melody; dark and ominous, but also beautiful. The powder caught fire and the rust-colored smoke filled the room.

When the chanting stopped, we lifted our hands to the sky, and the fire exploded, but it was like the smoke and the flames, all the energy in the room shot into my nose and mouth, hitting me right inside my chest. I was still standing, but I wouldn't be surprised if you told me Kiara died then and there.

"I told you it wasn't to be taken lightly," the woman warned, but there was more kindness to her now that it was done. She went to get a cup and filled it with boiling water and herbs, ushering me to take a seat.

"Is this a part of it?" Kiara asked of the Curse.

"This is for your nerves, your heart, and protection."

"I've never seen anything like them, Nell. There are hundreds of them, each driven mad with this quest for power. I've watched them die and come back to life, seen them murder without a second thought. If they unlock the powers, it will be hell on earth."

I finished my hot water and stood, taking a cylinder from my bag, that I handed to her.

"I don't want payment for this one," Nell argued, pushing it away.

"Take it as payment for the Cure then. Or as a thank you for always being there for me."

"I'll take it when you use it," she decided.

"Thank you, Nell. You're a loyal friend."

"Not a good one," she argued, but she still let me take her in for a hug.

I LEFT the wooden shack and walked along the road back to the church, but the world went fuzzy again, until I was in a stony cottage, my heart racing with fear. I also felt overwhelming pain, not from any wound that I could see, but from a primal place that tore through my heart and soul. I was holding a dagger in my right hand, while the left one rubbed my still-pregnant stomach. I took so many deep breaths, but nothing calmed me down in the least.

I stood in the middle of the room, facing the front door, ready. I couldn't hear anything other than my own heartbeat, pounding in my ears, but I could feel them. It was like when Donovan got to Embry's villa. I couldn't feel any individual person, but there was so much magic, more than I could even imagine, coming at me from all sides.

The closer they got, the more panicked Kiara became, her breathing more difficult, until the magic got closer than she was comfortable with. It moved faster, rushing at her. I looked out the window and saw an army of men, women, and creatures, ready to strike. My breathing calmed. I let out one last deep breath, then drove the dagger through my heart.

I WOKE up and heard screaming, then realized that it was me.

"Was it Kiara?" Embry asked, looking worried, but I was in Gabriel's arms, and he looked downright horrified. "What happened?"

The look in Gabriel's eyes told me that this was one of those times where I didn't just pass out, I acted parts of it out, so they knew exactly what happened.

"They were coming, and I knew I couldn't stop them. No matter how hard I fought, I was alone and there were so many of them, and they would do terrible things to so many people, and I didn't have any other choice," I said, Kiara's thoughts mixing with mine.

"Let's get you somewhere safe," Gabriel decided, lifting me up in his arms as if I weighed nothing. I wanted to tell him I was fine, that I could walk, so he really didn't have to... but I felt so safe in his arms that I let him.

CHAPTER SIXTEEN

We rented a room at another bed-and-breakfast. I think the guys liked their non-digitized check-in systems, but I worried that if anyone found us, the somewhat nosy proprietors might interfere and get hurt more than the minimum-wage employees at a chain hotel.

There was a coffeemaker on the bureau, so Embry made me some tea. I took a sip, feeling a chill despite being all bundled up on one of the double beds. My head was killing me, but I tried not to show it, keenly aware of their eyes on me.

"I'm sorry I reacted like that. I've seen worse." I tried to figure out why it hit me so hard, but I knew. Kiara not only gave up the fight and took her own life, she took her unborn child's.

"Seeing things isn't the same as living them," Gabriel assured me.

"I was Kiara, obviously, and she knew people were after her. She went to a witch who gave her both Kiara's Cure, and Kiara's Curse. The witch, Nell, she wasn't happy about it, but she cursed her. She said there would be unexpected consequences, but Kiara was prepared for that."

They gave me a moment to compose myself and keep going, but when I didn't, Embry asked, "What did the curse do?"

"I'm not sure, but she called it a sacrifice. The room filled with smoke, and it shot into me. I thought it killed me, but it didn't."

"But you did die, right?" Gabriel had the same look in his eyes from when I woke up in his arms.

"Not exactly. I could feel them coming, like Ingrid felt Donovan. They were so powerful and there were so many of them. She didn't have Gifted protectors, so when they got close enough…" I took a deep breath and closed my eyes before admitting, "She put the dagger through her own heart."

Gabriel put his hand on mine like he didn't really know what to say, but he could see there was more. And calling it her heart might be accurate, but I was still inside her when she did it.

"Your dagger?" Embry asked the least invasive of all the questions he must have.

"I don't think so." I shook my head. I was more concentrated on what was going on inside. "I know it's a long stretch, but I could bring us to the witch's place tomorrow in case there's anything." I didn't expect Nell to still be living there, but magic seemed to be something passed down through generations, so her grimoire might be there somewhere. Otherwise, I might get another memory, preferably of when Kiara asked for it, so I could know what the smoke did that was so terrible, compared to killing two birds with one dagger.

"First thing in the morning," Embry said, but they were both looking at me like I might break at any moment.

"I… she was pregnant," I admitted, wiping the warm tears that fell as I did. I didn't mean to be this affected, but I couldn't help it. I kept thinking of Cassie, who lost so many babies, and how broken Kiara was when she did it. "She said it was a boy, but I don't know how she would know…"

Gabriel gave my hand a squeeze and looked at me like he wanted to wrap me in his arms and take my pain away, but he couldn't. Embry let in a sharp breath and couldn't meet my eyes. I knew he was thinking of his son, Jackson, that they never thought they'd be able to have, who died before having a family of his own, like all the sons in my family.

"That was the consequence, wasn't it?" I asked, but it was mostly rhetorical. Kiara killed her son, so her descendants were cursed to endure heartache after heartache, as a reminder.

"You said she didn't have a choice." Gabriel emphasized the 'she' to remind me that although I was holding the knife and did it, I was just reliving a memory of something someone else did roughly five centuries ago.

"I don't know. She didn't think she did, but I don't know if she even tried running or fighting or if she just…"

"Gave up," Gabriel finished for me. I made the mistake of looking into his dark eyes, which were so intense that I nearly got lost in them. "You said it yourself that she didn't have us," he reminded me. "I will not let that happen to you. We will fight, we will run, and I will keep you safe."

"What if you can't?" I asked quietly, though I wanted so badly to believe him.

"That isn't an option," he said simply, but looking into those eyes, I trusted him.

"Why don't you get some sleep, and we'll start again in the morning?" Embry suggested, coming over to take the empty mug from me. He pulled down the bedsheets so I could climb in, then placed them back on top of me, along with the blankets I'd been bundled up in since we arrived.

He put his hand on mine and gave me an apologetic smile, but a calm washed over me. I knew exactly what he was doing, but for once I didn't mind. The headache disappeared, and I got so tired that I couldn't keep my eyes open. It was scary how quickly his Gift sent me into dreamland, but I prayed I wouldn't have any.

CHAPTER SEVENTEEN

I slept in the next morning, either naturally or because of Embry's Gift. I replaced my shock and sadness with a determination to sort this out and reverse the Curse before we lost more innocent lives. Not that I planned on getting pregnant and continuing the line while Henry still walked the earth, but if Gifted lore taught me anything, it's that some things are predetermined and there isn't much you can do to stop them.

EMBRY LED the way to the church's courtyard, then we followed the path Kiara took, basing my directions off of which way I had to turn rather than landmarks, because nothing looked the same. I still had the directions Father Dunn gave us, but now that I knew why Kiara was denied a proper burial, I wasn't sure I wanted to see it.

A cozy little tearoom with a chalkboard announcing the specials replaced the wooden shack from my memory. I stopped dead once I spotted it, causing Embry to nearly walk right into me.

"I think we're in luck," I said soberly.

"Which one is it?" they asked.

"The tearoom." I pointed, waiting for them to see the crescent moon logo above the shop's door.

"Or that's a scary coincidence," Embry tried. It was an exact replica of the one on the back of my neck, only it was sideways. You could argue it was the outline of a mug with three marshmallows inside, but I wasn't that naïve.

WIND CHIMES ANNOUNCED OUR ARRIVAL, but the tearoom was empty. This was a small town with few tourists, and we were hours early for afternoon tea. I was surprised by how small the room was, given the size of the building. I was looking for something supernatural or out of place, but I felt like there was more to the little shop.

"Welcome to the tearoom. Can I get you a cream tea, afternoon tea, or just regular tea?" The girl who came up to us was younger than me and clearly not the owner. We were interrupting her from whatever she'd been doing on her cell phone while walking over, and she was eager to serve us and get back to that.

"Cream tea has scones with jam and clotted cream, but afternoon tea has all the mini sandwiches and desserts," Embry told my confused look, because the waitress wasn't going to.

"Afternoon tea," I decided. The original plan was just to come by and ask questions, maybe look around a bit, but we had to eat anyway, and I doubted this girl knew anything.

"Is this a family business?" I asked after the guys ordered the same.

"Not mine," she told me. "Miss Duncan is in the kitchen baking."

"Do you think I could ask her some questions? Once she's done baking."

"I'll tell her you asked," she assured me before going to put in our orders.

"I haven't had afternoon tea in at least a century." Embry looked excited, but it was possibly just for my benefit.

"Delia likes to drag me to these whenever I'm in town." Gabriel looked around the room like he was both comparing it to the other tearooms, and scoping out the security threats.

"I always thought it was the pinnacle of sophistication. I loved the idea of drinking tea and having an excuse to try every dessert they put in front of you."

"That's because you chose not to do cotillion." Embry stopped me from feeling sorry for myself.

"Have you been to those things?" I asked, but Embry shook his head. "I looked at the pamphlets. You learn how to do things like a proper lady, which sounded fun, but then you get introduced to society as the daughter of so and so, accompanied by so and so. I had one guy who talked to me in high school, but not so much that he would escort me to something like that. And Daughter of Unknown just doesn't have the right ring to it."

"I would have proudly claimed you, as I'm sure Sam would have," Embry told me. I caught Gabriel in the corner of my eye, looking down at his plate. The realist in me figured he was trying not to hurt my feelings by not volunteering to do the same, but the optimist wondered if he would want to be the one to escort me, should the opportunity come up again.

"I doubt it would have helped with anything now." I shrugged it off.

"Here's your tea." The waitress put a large teapot in the middle of the table, where there was a small ceramic milk pot and a bowl with cubes of sugar inside. "Miss Duncan said she'd be happy to come 'round later."

"Thank you." I gave her a smile before pouring out the tea. I added one of the brown sugar cubes and milk to mine. This was one experience I had looked forward to when reading about them or watching movies, but real life wasn't measuring up. The tea was delicious, so that wasn't it, but even though this was nothing like the wooden shack, I still felt very uneasy. The entire purpose of the trip also put a damper on any sightseeing or experiences we were having.

"Is any of it familiar?" Embry caught my mood.

"No, everything is different. When I came it was a wooden shack; every surface had jars or vials with powders and liquids… there was a big fire over there, but it wasn't any bigger than that." I used my arms to designate a corner of the shop.

"Which means the crescent is new."

"Or the coffee cup," I agreed. "Do you know any Gifted named Duncan?"

"I know a guy whose first name is Duncan, but no one from around here," Gabriel shared.

"What can Duncan do?" I asked, mostly as a distraction.

"He took voices." There was an edge to Gabriel's.

"Like Ursula in the Little Mermaid?" I asked.

"Maybe?" Gabriel looked unsure, as if he hadn't seen the movie.

"This wasn't a friend," I read his look. Not to mention, Duncan's Gift implied he took advantage of people.

"He was a slaveowner in his first life, and a scream trader in every life after that."

"Scream trader?" I pressed.

"I never asked." He looked away, giving me the impression he was lying.

"Here are some scones with our homemade clotted cream and fig jam." The waitress gave each of us two scones, then went back to the kitchen and her cell phone.

I watched Gabriel put his clotted cream first, then a spoonful of fig jam to each half, while Embry spread the jam on one half and clotted cream on the other. Embry put the whole thing together like a sandwich, but Gabriel savored one half at a time, so I followed his lead.

"This is delicious," I said after my first bite.

"They're pretty good as far as scones go," Embry agreed.

"Afternoon tea for three." The woman who carried out the multi-tiered plates was about fifty years old with the same long, blonde curly hair as Nell, only she had it all tied up in a bun. "I heard you had some questions?"

"My... my grandmother came here a long time ago, so I was wondering if this has been in your family for a long time." As I said it, it occurred to me how unlikely it would be that she was related to the woman who owned a wooden shack here centuries ago, but I still had that feeling.

"Since the sixteenth century," she agreed with a warm smile. "It hasn't always been a café though. We used to sell trinkets and souvenirs, but this isn't the most touristic area."

"I like the logo." Embry mirrored her smile, so it sounded like a compliment, but he was fishing.

"Funny story." She smiled to herself. "The old shop used to have this moon and stars logo, which was ridiculous when we sold nothing related to astronomy. Or astrology. I can never tell those two apart, but we didn't have either of them here. Anyway, on the day the shop became mine, the sign fell. Only one end came loose, so it was hanging sideways above the doorway. I thought it looked like a coffee cup, and this place was born."

"That's interesting," I said it with a smile, but the idea that my birthmark was their shop's logo gave me pause. "When you say the shop became yours..."

"Oh, my parents died in a car crash after my grandparents retired, so it all came to me," she said it fast, in that way I sometimes did so people wouldn't pity me for my tragic life story.

"I'm so sorry," I said.

"It was a long time ago, dear," she assured me. "Did your grandmother want you to pick something up for her?"

"I was hoping to find out more about this place in the

sixteenth century." I tried to seem nonchalant, wondering how to find out where she stood on the supernatural without scaring her away.

"My grandmother could have told you all about it. I have some city stills of life back then if you'd like," she offered.

"City stills?"

"I don't know what else to call them, but I have five or six paintings upstairs, each one is just people living their day-to-day life."

"Painted now, or..."

"Then," she answered for me while heading to a staircase. She looked surprised that the guys followed, but didn't stop them. "My ancestor used to brew homemade remedies and stuff, with her customers paying in trades. One of them gave paintings and poems, though I'm not sure if they were all for remedies, or just as gifts."

"Is this that ancestor?" I asked, the portrait of Nell sticking out among all the cityscapes.

"This is the one that makes me think they were friends," she agreed.

"You say she brewed home remedies?" I probed.

"Remedies, potions, spells... whatever the people needed," she agreed.

I turned to her in shock, but she brought over a large volume open to a handmade drawing of Kiara.

"You're one as well?" I asked.

"Very minimally, but I felt it as soon as you came in. I wasn't sure you were her until I checked the book," she explained.

"What do you know about me?" I looked back at the guys who both tensed up, not as trusting as I was.

"You're in the grimoire that's passed down through the generations of my family. Nell wrote ninety percent of it, with a few spells added in along the way."

"What does it say?"

"It has Kiara's Curse and Kiara's Cure," she said, flipping through the pages. "But you're not Kiara, obviously."

"Lucy," I agreed. "Does it say what the Curse was?"

"Have any of the Bearers lived past twenty-eight?"

"No." I shook my head.

"After Kiara died, Nell added a paragraph with the drawing. The 'Curse' bound Kiara's Coalescent powers so the people hunting her couldn't get them, but provided a failsafe in case they did."

"How come she stabbed herself if the spell would have killed her?"

"The Curse works however it needs to. And from what I understand of the Prophecy, if she hadn't pierced through her heart, as long as they showed up within a few minutes, they would have been able to use it."

"Would you have anything of hers?" I asked, not needing her to confirm that our lack of male heirs was also because of the curse.

"Just the paintings." She shrugged, looking around at all the cityscapes.

"They're all hers?" I looked around as well.

"There's also a canvas in a preservation tube upstairs. It was payment for the Curse, and Nell refused to open it until Kiara used the cure. I never had that much self-restraint, but it felt wrong to hang it up," she shared. "It's yours if you want it."

"I would be eternally grateful," I told her as Embry took money out.

"That's not necessary," she told him. "We've spent generations trying to get rid of it without Nell cursing us for it, but I think she would approve of this. I'm guessing it's hard to track down objects belonging to women who died centuries ago?"

"It is," I agreed. "But this really helps."

"You look like you've got a few years to figure it out," she tried to reassure me.

"Of course." She didn't need to know that I had doubts about making it through the week these days. "You wouldn't know how many Bearers came before Kiara, would you?" I eyed the volume that was open to the Cure page.

"I would guess… two," she said after counting under her breath. "Nell's spells all have ingredient counts at the bottom, and this one has nine. That's daffodil, sage, aloe, bezoar, honey water, something from her mother and her father, which leaves two for the Bearers that came before her."

"What's that?" I asked, noticing another scribble that wasn't on my copy either.

"It's Nell's handwriting… it just says veil with a question mark."

"Did she often scribble on spells?"

"It probably has something to do with Kiara, but I couldn't tell you what."

"Thank you so much. You've been incredibly helpful."

"It's what we're here for." She gave me a smile.

"Is there a reason the logo was a crescent moon with stars?" I asked as we were heading out.

"The crescent symbolizes life and death, fertility, womanhood… old Nell thought it represented her skills, since most people those days came here to get pregnant, to get rid of an unwanted pregnancy, or to poison people. I don't think she actually helped those last ones, but historically, that's what people wanted."

"Thank you again," I told her before following the guys outside.

I got a flash of Kiara spotting the symbol painted on a rock outside the wooden shack and knocking with a smile, convinced she found a kindred spirit.

CHAPTER EIGHTEEN

We waited until we were at the hotel before opening the preservation tube, as she called it. It was a lot newer than the one Kiara had given Nell, which told me they took care of it, even if they wanted nothing to do with it.

"Should we leave it inside to protect it?" I asked, feeling nervous as Embry slowly removed the canvas from its casing. As the painter among us, we figured he was best suited for the task.

"This is the best we're likely to find for Kiara, but it might have a clue or something to point us in the direction of the first Bearers, if we are to believe Mrs. Duncan," Embry pointed out.

"And we need the object, it doesn't matter if it falls apart," Gabriel reassured my nerves as Embry unrolled it.

At first, I thought it would be another city still, because I could only see the side of a stone house. But as he gently unrolled the canvas, it revealed a family. I would bet money that the laughing little girl was Saoirse, and the man her father.

"I think home would definitely mean a lot to her," I said, since my primary concern for the painting was whether it meant something to her.

"But it doesn't tell us anything about the women who came before her." Embry sighed, disappointed.

"If we're down to two, it's just the ones mentioned in Beth's book that had the Prophecy."

"Any idea where we find them?" Embry asked me.

"I hoped we would figure that out by working our way backwards, but I still have no idea who Saint Malachy or Talina and Zeke are." I looked from one to the other, who both shook their heads.

"Remind me exactly what the book said?" Gabriel asked.

"Something about the first mention of the Prophecy was in 1148 by Saint Malachy, talking about the miraculous light of angels." I tried to remember the exact words, but other than the names I wrote down, all I had were bits and pieces. "Then the actual spell was written in the part about Talina and Zeke, who apparently ruled from 1385 to 1460."

"Let's find their kingdom." Embry decided, guiding us to the local library.

THE KINGDOM of Talina and Zeke turned out to be a rather large island off the coast of Spain. It was known as La Isla de la Luna Encantada, or the Island of the Enchanted Moon, which told me we were definitely headed in the right direction. According to the one book we found that mentioned it, a tsunami destroyed a large part of the island a couple hundred years ago, leaving only a small part of the majesty it once was. The book was from the sixties, so probably not the most accurate information, but it said there were still over twenty thousand people living on the island.

We flew a commercial flight to Spain, then took a boat to the island. I didn't want to take any chances with the Ocean waves, so I slowly sipped water with crushed ginger and lemon, keeping my eyes on the land in the distance.

"It'll help calm your stomach," Gabriel explained, handing me a pack of saltine crackers.

"Thank you." I gave him a grin, feeling ridiculous to be so affected by seasickness. "I'm sorry you can't hide me away from lurking eyes in one of the cabins below deck."

"As long as they wait until we're on dry land to attack, we should be good." He gave me a teasing smile.

"This is another time where levitating myself would have come in handy," I pointed out.

"I think I'd rather have you seasick than have to explain to everyone on this ship how come you're floating above them."

"Now you're just being difficult," I warned.

"My apologies, please continue with your marvelous plan."

"Thank you," I said graciously, but that was the extent of it. "Are you going to tell me this is also a plain landscape full of awful memories?" I turned the focus to the island that was coming a lot quicker than Ireland had.

"No, this is my first time in Spain. It reminds me of a cross between Italy and New Mexico."

"Warm and colorful with Latin influences?"

"Exactly," he agreed. "I would love to draw it."

"Why don't you?"

"I'm working," he said dismissively.

"We're traveling. And although Embry is sitting with the bags, he's diligently staring at me and checking everyone out."

"I don't have my pencils," he argued.

"All I'm hearing are excuses."

He looked at me, considering it, before going to get some paper from my backpack.

"That's bold," I said of the pen he chose to draw with.

"Your mechanical pencil was too thin and barely had an eraser," he explained.

We kept up a stream of conversation, with lengthy pauses whenever he was concentrating hard. I could tell because his forehead creased, and he bit on his bottom lip. I found myself staring when he was looking down, but caught myself before he looked up at the scenery again.

"Oh, that's just beautiful," a woman said, stopping to look over Gabriel's shoulder. If I were him, my first instinct would have been to cover my work and close myself off, but the woman had Grams' smile and Charlie's kind eyes.

"Thank you." Gabriel gave her a shy smile. I could swear he was blushing.

"We've been watching you from over there and we think you make the loveliest couple." She looked over at me while her friend came to join her. Both women were nearing their nineties, but while the first woman had white hair, the second's was dyed flaming red.

"We're not a couple," I corrected her when Gabriel stayed silent.

"Shouldn't be too long," Embry interrupted, coming to stand beside me. I saw him watching from afar earlier, but I guess he felt the need to come close when the women lingered.

"Oh, I'm so sorry, I was sure..." the first woman apologized, looking from Gabriel to Embry with confusion.

I wanted to tell her it wasn't like that with Embry either, even less actually, but the two women walked off as our ship got close to shore. The closer we got, the more a weird feeling overcame me. It wasn't like when someone powerful was close... it was like the whole island was made of magic.

CHAPTER NINETEEN

Our first stop was the island's museum, since we were coming here mostly clueless as to who Talina and Zeke were. The rest of the island inhabitants, on the other hand, honored them on every street corner. The manhole covers all featured an elaborate intertwining of 'T&Z'.

"It's $12.50." A girl my age was behind the desk when we walked in. She looked like she was falling asleep while working on math homework.

Embry took the money out of his pocket and paid for the three of us.

"Is there a guide or something we can get as well?" I asked when she handed him the change.

"We have a coloring guide we give to kids when the schools come, but you mostly just walk around and read the stuff on the walls."

THE MUSEUM WENT through the entire history of the island, with a 'step into the past' theme. Which meant we started with the present-day politics and economics, going further and further back in time.

"We're getting close," I pointed out when we reached the painting of the Island's first democratically elected President, a Spanish woman who came to the island as a child when they hired her mother to teach. The book Beth was reading said Talina and Zeke ruled before her, from 1385 to 1460, which was a really long time.

"While a majority elected her, it took a long time for some of the elders to warm up to her, as she was the one who encouraged the Crowned Princess Ilana to travel to the mainland, where she fell in love and never returned," Embry read the description.

"You're emphasizing the last part instead of how exceptional it is that this island, in the fifteenth century, held democratic elections. And a woman won."

"Talina gave up her crown when she lost Zeke. She trained her replacement before living out a quiet life in her country house," Gabriel suggested as a possible location to find things.

"I think everything valuable is in here," I argued, moving closer to the glass cases in the middle of the room. They held objects that showed how people lived under Talina and Zeke's rule, but the star of the show seemed to be a large, faded brown book open to a page full of squiggles I couldn't really make out, even if I'd understood the language.

"Who's Ioanit?" Gabriel read over my shoulder.

"Their historian," I shared, feeling his breath on the back of my neck.

"Nothing here actually belonged to them."

"Except for that." I nodded to the coronet they forged specifically for Talina. Apparently, instead of passing down the crown, a new one was made for each ruler, with the previous one keeping theirs. It was more surprising that the position seemed to be passed on when the current ruler chose to step down rather than upon their death, as in every other country throughout history.

"Nothing smaller?" He asked.

"I think they'll notice if we leave with the crown," I argued when I caught on.

"Coronet. Because it's smaller," Embry pointed out.

"Not that small. We can't take it," I whispered, looking around to see if the place had any security cameras.

"It's not stealing, it's borrowing. If the spell doesn't destroy it, we can bring it back," Embry reminded me.

"We'll have to come back tomorrow morning," I reluctantly agreed to their plan.

"And not right now because…"

"I think going to jail will put a huge damper on our plans."

"You're a witch," Gabriel reminded me.

"Yes, but once we leave the museum, we have to hide out on the island until the next boat, that leaves tomorrow morning."

"I'm glad someone read the ferry schedule." They gave up on trying to make the heist happen tonight.

CHAPTER TWENTY

Embry told us he had some potential leads he wanted to look into, so Gabriel and I were alone for supper on a gorgeous island. I knew he would want to keep me locked up in a hotel room to be safe, but I had a plan.

"We can pick up burgers or a pizza on the way to a hotel." He was clearly paying more attention to the people than the buildings because I hadn't seen a single American food chain. Even restaurants were few and far between; all mom-and-pop shops from what I could tell.

"Or we can try to find an alternative to stealing the most valuable item in that museum," I suggested.

"Do you have an idea where we should look?"

"All the guidebooks say that if you want to get to know a place, you ask the locals."

"We're trying to lie low and not let everyone on this island know that we're travelers from America looking into Crescent Moon Bearers and a long-forgotten dynasty," Gabriel argued.

"We stick out like a sore thumb. As soon as we got off here instead of the party island, we became gossip. If someone wanted to know we were here, they already know."

"Can you sense anyone?" He kept leaning in and speaking softly, to prevent people from overhearing him, but every time his fingers accidentally brushed mine, I had to resist the urge to hold them.

"This entire island is giving off some mega-vibes, but they seem peaceful, if that makes any sense."

"Not really, but let me know if that changes." He gave me the tiniest of smiles before we walked towards where the royal house used to be. The majority of it was destroyed along with most of the island, but there was a tiny part of it that still stood at the northernmost end. History books had led me to believe that kingdoms comprised a castle surrounded by their city, with the whole thing encompassed by impenetrable stone walls. According to movies, the only way in or out was a drawbridge, because water always surrounded them.

This kingdom either didn't have enemies, or they trusted the outer layer of tiny walls to keep their attackers out. At least to slow them down as they hopped over it.

"Anything?" Gabriel asked when I sat on the wall, that barely reached my waist, and put my hands on its stones.

"Nope." I shrugged, looking around for talismans or discarded jewels on the ground, knowing neither was likely.

"It's beautiful, isn't it?" he said of the waves crashing on the beach.

"It must have been paradise once upon a time," I ventured.

"I always knew you came from a line of strong, capable women."

"You didn't know it went this far," I called him on it.

"No, but I am not at all surprised to find that your ancestors ran a matriarchal kingdom that saw centuries of peace and prosperity."

"It's a lot for anyone to live up to." I thought of Kiara's mother, Ilana, and wondered if it was more than love that made her want to leave the island.

"This is where you come from, Lucy. This light and strength and greatness; that's who you are."

I gave him a smile instead of answering. I knew what he meant, and I definitely came from some impressive women, but I couldn't just forget about the other contributions.

The wind blew my hair into my face, so I brought my hand up to tuck it behind my ear. When I brought my hand back to the stone wall, I accidentally put it on Gabriel's. I was going to take it away and apologize, but he didn't move his hand away. He said nothing, so I left mine on his, and for a moment, we just sat there, staring out at the ocean, almost hand in hand.

THE SUN WAS SETTING, so we walked back to civilization, choosing a pizza place for our dinner, but it was nothing like the delivery pizza he'd originally suggested. The crust was paper thin, covered in olive oil, spinach, mushrooms, and tomato. I added cheese to mine and Gabriel had sun-dried tomatoes on his.

"Interesting," I commented, biting into my heavenly slice.

"Embry's mother used to preserve tomatoes by leaving them out in the sun, but every time she did, squirrels took at least a quarter of them." He was the picture of innocence.

"She knew it was you."

"You never even met her," he argued, more because he wanted to hear my argument than because he thought I was wrong.

"She would have put something on top to prevent it, or added spices to them ahead of laying them out. She let it happen because she knew it was you. Mrs. Boyd used to smile at Mr. Boyd and say the birds came through the window and ate the cookies she had on the counter, but she knew he was the one who took them."

"Mrs. Dante was a very honest woman," he defended her with a smile.

"Sometimes, to make the people you love happy, you tell yourself stories." I shrugged.

"Or keep things from them," he tried.

"Lie to them, you mean?" We were talking about us now. "I understand lying to people when the truth is something that will hurt them, but not when it's vital information that determines whether they live or die and who they can trust and..." I cut myself off, but put my hand out so he wouldn't respond yet. "It hurt me that you didn't feel you could trust me with the truth. That even after everything, you still see me as a child who can't deal with the hard things, but I am not. I passed middle-age years ago," I tried to make it less serious with a joke about my impending doom.

"We will fix that," he told me like there was no other option, but that was far from being the case. The lie was more for him than to me, so I let it slide. "And I know you're not a child, Lucy. I wish I didn't. I wish I could tell you to stay back and hide, and that you would listen and be safe. Not that I don't trust you with the truth, it's that I want to protect you from it. To save you from whatever pain or sadness that I can. Not because I think you're too young to handle it, but because you lie to make the people you love happy." He went back to eating his slice of pizza like that wasn't a heated declaration that gave me butterflies. I don't think Gabriel had told me he loved me before. Ever.

"I thought your job was to keep me safe, not happy." I don't know why I felt the need to prod instead of taking the win, but I had a bad feeling that Henry would catch up with us soon, and I didn't want to have regrets when we failed.

"You're right," he agreed. "I'm here to protect you. Rather your heart. Which means more than not letting someone cut it out, or stopping you from running a dagger through it."

"I'm not planning on that," I argued, going back to my pizza.

"No, but you're willing to. If we get to a point where you don't think we'll win, you're prepared to sacrifice yourself."

"Better than sacrificing someone else for my curse."

"Who are you to tell me who I'm allowed to give my life for?"

"Who are you to tell me?" I countered.

"I come back," he pointed out.

"How are the pizzas?" The man who ran the kitchen chose that moment to come out and talk to us.

"Delicious." I gave him a smile, but Gabriel was still looking pointedly at me.

"How long are you in town for?"

"We leave in the morning," I shared.

"Short visit." He shook his head and pressed his lips together like it was a shame.

"It's a quick trip, but I wanted to find out more about Talina and Zeke," I gave him an opening.

"You saw the museum?" he asked.

"We did."

"Then you know the official stuff."

"Is there unofficial stuff?" I leaned forward in my chair, causing the man to make a big-bellied chuckle.

"I was born here, then went to school in London. Instead of retiring, I came back here and opened a pizza parlor because this is the only place in the world where I wouldn't lock my doors, would lend a stranger my car, and have never felt unsafe," he shared.

"The museum mentioned a low crime rate," I agreed, feeling guilty about our plans.

"It's not just low, it's nonexistent. I don't know if it's the island or the lifestyle, but we honor Talina, Xiomara, and all the ones who turned us into this instead of that." He pointed across the ocean, to Europe.

"I need to live here to know the unofficial stuff," I understood.

"Tonight might be a good start." He nodded to the sky, where a firework went off.

"What's tonight?" Gabriel asked.

"It's Luna Creciente."

"The Crescent Moon?" Gabriel translated, although I would have guessed it even if I didn't take Spanish in high school.

"Not for a few days, but tonight's the opening of the festival. There'll be fireworks and dancing… it lasts all week, if you can stay a little longer."

"No, we really need to leave, but thank you."

WE SETTLED our bill and headed off to the hotel to tell Embry. Islanders crowded the streets for the festival, so Gabriel took my hand and brought me through a quieter alley instead.

"I think it's the island," I suggested. "I mean, not to take away from my ancestors, but the energy I'm getting from it is like… it feels very wholesome," I tried to explain it.

"I was going to say hopeful," he agreed instead of telling me I was crazy. "You're enjoying it, but it terrifies me."

"Being hopeful?" I asked, very aware that he hadn't let go of my hand yet. Recent events had me uncomfortable in crowds and in dark alleys, so I appreciated it for more reasons than one.

"Hope can be dangerous," he pointed out. "I feel like I can do things I would normally stop myself from doing."

"Things you would regret?"

"No, but I probably should." He looked over at me, his black eyes piercing in the moonlight, making my breath catch.

"You think everyone on the island gets along because they all feel buzzed?" I had never been drunk, so I didn't know what it was supposed to feel like, but I was pretty sure this wasn't it.

"No, it's not like being drunk. Alcohol lowers your inhibitions and prevents you from thinking things through. I can see all the consequences my actions could have, all the implications… but they seem worth it. Like a weird optimism that has me believing that good things can happen, and I deserve them. It's very strange."

"What actions?" I asked. He was looking at me in a way that

told me I knew what he was referring too, but he was sharing so much that I couldn't believe he would be that open about something we'd only ever mentioned in subtext before.

"I can't tell you that, Luce," he said, but his eyes told me everything.

"You can tell me anything, remember?"

"I'm supposed to protect your heart," he argued.

We weren't walking anymore. We were both standing in the alley, looking straight into each other's eyes, lit only by the moon. My heart was pounding in a way that made me want to scream, or to reach out and kiss him, but the only thing worse than not acting on these feelings would be if I did something and lost him for it.

"Sometimes keeping things from the people you love doesn't make them happy," I warned, biting on my bottom lip, hyperaware of how he was now holding both of my hands, and how he kept looking down at my lips.

I could see the battle going on in his mind; his head against his heart. I was rooting for his heart with every fiber of my being, trying to act normal while I was screaming inside.

"It's funny, I never realized I was getting over her, never felt my feelings dim or the pain grow smaller, but one day, I saw you walking towards me and I just knew."

"You knew what?" I asked, feeling nervous, even though this was Gabriel, and I had dreamed of this moment so many times over the summer.

"That I loved you," he admitted. He said it simply, not like he expected anything in return, but he didn't mean it like I loved Sam or Embry. He meant the way he had loved Annabelle. "I was broken long before you smiled at me on your eighteenth birthday and took my breath away. For the first time in what felt like forever, my heart came alive, and I wanted those things I thought I would never get to have. But I knew that I shouldn't, that you deserved better. That's why I stayed away, hoping the feelings would disappear, but as soon as you crawled out of the bathroom window and barreled into me, it all came back. I tried to be distant, to stay in the woods at the plantation so I wouldn't betray myself and lose you, but... I love you." Suddenly, before I realized what was happening, Gabriel leaned in, his hand pulling my face closer to his. Our lips were inches away when he paused, giving me the chance to back away if I wanted to, but I didn't. I moved closer, just as he did, so our lips touched. I felt the tingling all the way down to my toes. It was like I didn't know I was drowning until he pulled me up and I could breathe again.

A new string of fireworks surprised me with their loud bangs, closer to us than they had been earlier, but as soon as Gabriel made sure it wasn't a danger to us, he laughed at my reaction. It was a childish laugh, full of innocence that made me smile before leaning in and kissing him back. I half-expected him to push me away, like every other time I got close, but he caressed my cheek and looked at me like he never wanted to let me go.

EMBRY HAD ALREADY RENTED the rooms for us; two with an adjoining door. Gabriel didn't let go of my hand the entire walk there, which included lots of detours, sparks, and fireworks.

When we got to the room, he stopped and pulled me close, kissing me one last time before knocking so Embry could let us in. It felt like I lost a part of me when he let go of my hand, but later, when we brushed our teeth side by side, he gave me a smile, the kind where as hard as you try, you can't stop smiling. I could tell this wasn't just a one-time thing. It was the start of something wonderful.

CHAPTER TWENTY-ONE

We checked out the next morning and headed straight for the museum. Our plan was to have Embry distract the person behind the desk while Gabriel and I got the coronet. Whatever Embry had done last night told him that the museum had no security guards or cameras, which made sense with what the man from the pizzeria told us. The information slightly lowered the fear factor of the mission, but greatly increased my guilt.

"It was definitely blue," I told Gabriel as soon as we walked into the museum, our entrance fees already in my hand. It would have been more realistic to try and get in for free to check out one tiny detail, but I felt better paying twenty-five dollars for the coronet rather than just taking it.

"It was green. I know because I thought it was an emerald at first." Gabriel played along to perfection, but I tried not to look surprised. I knew the guys could lie, but wasn't aware they could act.

"Then maybe you're colorblind," I told him before turning to the girl, who was still doing homework. "Us again. Two tickets, please. It'll be worth it to see your face when you realize that I'm right," I said the last part to Gabriel.

"Um, sure. Go on in." She looked equally surprised that she had visitors, and that it was us. Again.

"This is what the entire trip has been like…"

I could hear Embry being his charming self with her, but I focused on our part of the mission.

"I'll get rid of the glass for you, but if anyone catches us, you need to leave me behind," I told Gabriel.

"Not happening," he argued.

"I can talk my way out of whatever happens, especially with Embry there, but we won't have another chance at the coronet, and that's what we're here for," I reminded him it wasn't about me sacrificing myself, it was just logic. "It's not like they can do much to us if you leave with the evidence."

He looked like he wanted to point out all the ways that wasn't true, but didn't want to worry me, so he nodded and took my hand to bring me to the room with the coronet. We both pretended we were looking for the stone on the spine of Ioanit's book.

We put a lot more into the cover story than we needed, but I chose the perfect place where I would have an unobstructed view of the coronet's display case, but no one could accuse me of stealing it from so far away.

"See, I told you it was blue," I said, my voice shaky. Gabriel looked at me to see if I was ready, then gave my hand a squeeze. I didn't have as much confidence in myself as I implied, but a few moments after I held the moonstone necklace and concentrated on the case, it disappeared. One second, I was smiling with pride for accomplishing a new spell, and the next the coronet was gone. I let out the breath I was holding, then let the glass materialize back in its place.

"It was a trick of the light." Gabriel gave me a reassuring look before heading to the exit.

His version of leaving me behind consisted of walking two steps ahead of me and not stopping once we got to the front desk.

My heart was beating a mile a minute, but I tried to appear calm, cool, and collected in case Embry was wrong and a delayed alarm went off. It would have been smarter to get a forgery to replace it with, because they would find us out the second someone else visited the museum. I wondered if I should tell someone it was missing, or ask what happened to it, just for plausible deniability.

Embry was waiting by the doors, so I took another calming breath before joining him.

"He was wrong," I explained Gabriel's quick exit.

Embry and I were about to walk out when the girl behind the desk called out, "Miss!"

I froze, terrified. There had to be some kind of morality code against using magic to steal things, which meant I definitely couldn't use it on this girl to save us from being caught.

I took a deep breath to steady myself before turning to face her. "Yes?" I asked, every inch of me stiff from trying to appear normal.

"I found one of the coloring guides we give the kids, if you still want it," she offered.

"Thank you so much." I swallowed before retracing my steps to get the guide from her.

"Have a great day." She sighed and went back to her homework.

I waited until we were outside to freak out, but for someone who never even skipped school or stole so much as a chocolate bar, I felt like I may have just had a heart attack.

. . .

GABRIEL WAS STANDING across the street with the coronet safe in his jacket pocket.

"Everything okay?" he asked, putting a hand on my arm.

"We made it." I tried to smile, but I wasn't there yet. I was guessing it would take being back on American soil before my heartbeat went back to normal. It was crazy how stealing got me this nervous after all the magic stuff I had done in the past few months. Then again, stealing has always been wrong in the world I grew up in, whereas being hunted and nearly dying is so far-fetched I sometimes have trouble wrapping my head around it.

"We need to get out of here and board the ship before anyone notices the coronet is missing," Embry stated, looking back at the museum, where I half-expected a SWAT team to be rushing out at us.

"Here you go." Gabriel came close to hand me the coronet, away from potential prying eyes, but he held me extra close, as if to reassure me that I didn't just imagine last night. I was grateful, because as soon as I wrapped my hand around the little crown, I felt myself slipping…

MY HAIR WAS LONGER than I had ever seen it, cascading down my back, all the way to my hips. I felt like a Greek goddess, amplified by the incredibly fine, empire-waist silk gown I was wearing. There was a woman standing in front of me with a smile on her face, and a crowd of people surrounding us. Most of them were smiling too, some with the same love I felt from her, while others with curious excitement.

"Today my baby girl Talina turns eighteen," she addressed the crowd, but finished with a warm smile to me. "When I was little, my mother raised me to be strong and fierce. To be the best warrior, because you should never expect of your people something you wouldn't expect of yourself."

I recognized the coronet in her hand, shinier than the current version from the museum, but recognizable nonetheless. This one also seemed to have carvings in it, though I couldn't make them out from this far away.

"She was a force to be reckoned with," a very tall man added with a laugh, looking at the woman speaking – Talina's mother – in a way that suggested he might be her husband.

"True. But she was also warm and vulnerable. Because we are not just warriors, we are the mothers of our people. We tend to our sick, we comfort our dying, and we nurture our children to be kind and compassionate above all else. These are traits the world has convinced us to hide, but it is not weakness to fall apart. It is a chance to rebuild yourself and grow stronger, though most won't understand. When you put your heart in the game, others will see it as weakness, but it means you will fight harder and longer than anyone else. If something matters to you, my love, be all in," she told me with a fierce determination. "Courage isn't blindly running into danger without fear. Courage lies in seeing the danger, knowing what can happen, and going in regardless. Because there are things worth fighting for." She looked to the man who had interjected earlier. "But there are also things worth laying down your weapons for, and a queen must recognize the difference. This crown does not make you better than anyone, it marks you as the heart and soul of the kingdom."

I listened with fascination, but all I could feel in Talina was love. For her mother, for her people... her heart was bursting with it.

"I promise to rule justly, as a voice of reason when needed, but mostly, to be one of you. To be a friend and neighbor, through good times and bad, so we all may prosper and live happily ever after." As Talina said the last words, she looked to a man in the crowd who smiled at her in a way that made her heart flutter and her knees go weak. I would guess it was Zeke, but he didn't take part in the ceremony today. He was just one bystander among many. Talina smiled to him, then accepted her crown without fear, or even a trace of imposter syndrome. She didn't see it as her birthright, but as an honor she couldn't wait to begin. She made eye contact with every person in that crowd, giving each one her love and

respect. Her eyes landed on Zeke, and I could hear in the back of her mind, her mother warning her it was okay to want someone at your side, that the right person will strengthen you, but you should never need to have anyone else there....

CHAPTER TWENTY-TWO

"We have got to stop meeting like this." Gabriel smiled down at me when I opened my eyes.

"Where are we?" I tried to get up.

"Two men carrying an unconscious young woman wouldn't look good, so Embry went to get us tickets before the cutoff, and we are in an alley waiting for you to wake up," he explained.

"Passing out on the street was too risky, but a man with an unconscious woman in a dark alley seemed safe?" I questioned his logic.

"People expect shady things to happen in alleys. They don't question it as much." He looked like he was taking me in and definitely had me blushing.

"Thank you for catching me." I swallowed, smiling both because I was shy under his gaze, and because the nearness of him made me smile.

"Anytime." He brought me back up to a standing position but kept me close, and leaned in for a short, sweet kiss.

"The boat leaves in twenty minutes," I said after checking my watch. I wanted to ask him what this was, to figure out what we would tell Embry, but I didn't. Gabriel looked at me like there wasn't even an ounce of him that regretted his decision, but I couldn't help but worry the island really did put everyone on it under some magical spell of love and optimism that would all disappear once we reached the mainland.

"We have time then," he teased. He leaned in but let me bridge the last inch before a kiss that made me weak in the knees. From now on, that was the only reason I wanted to be fainting into people's arms. "We should board. Wouldn't want to be here when they realize it's missing."

"Always the voice of reason."

As I finished the last word, I felt a negative energy, like when Donovan had come to New Orleans. It was much weaker, but also like the entire positive vibe of the island got upset at it.

"Get behind me." Gabriel pulled me to him as the sky went dark and four people appeared in front of us. "Go to the ship," he told me.

"What's missing?" The person closest to us was a woman, but she was wearing a trench coat, with a hat covering most of her face. It was jarring to see Henry's army in anything other than black.

"Who are you?" I stepped out from behind Gabriel and put my hands up with my palms facing them, ready to use my powers if they made a move.

"Is 'Your Worst Nightmare' too much of a cliché?" she asked the person to her left, as I felt a chill behind me. I turned to see four more people blocking the exit Gabriel wanted me to take.

"If it's accurate, I say go with it." Her friend had a look in his eyes like he wanted to rip us to pieces, and he would enjoy it.

I was pretty sure that the way they were making jokes meant that they were here of their own free will, not being manipulated by Henry, but I didn't know the logistics of his control, and so far, only two of them were talking.

"We'll take the girl, and no harm will come to you," the woman told Gabriel. Something about her voice felt like a hammer against my skull, but I tried to shake it off.

"Over my dead body," he said through clenched teeth.

"It would be my pleasure to arrange that for you." She braced herself with her arms mirroring mine, only when she moved them, icy air surrounded us, like she was summoning a blizzard.

She brought her arms down and although I didn't know what she was throwing at us, I knew it wasn't good, so I put up my force shield. It kept us safe from the avalanche she poured on us, but the weight was going to crush me if I didn't push it off.

"The first chance you get, I need you to run." Gabriel looked me in the eyes with that look of utter intensity, laced with fear.

Instead of answering, I shot my arms up to push off the snow, but they were expecting it. As soon as I lifted my force shield, jets of hail, sparks, and weapons flew at us from different directions, making Gabriel and I separate to avoid being hit.

Gabriel pulled knives out of nowhere and got to work, brandishing one and throwing the others. I tried to freeze as many assailants as I could, but it was like they knew the limitations of my magic and operated around them. Instead of coming at me from one direction, they came from everywhere, making me constantly defend myself instead of being able to take the offensive.

I had two of them frozen, but the third one's Gift seemed to be popping in and out of places, so one minute he was behind me, the next he was beside me and so on. His weapon felt like a baseball bat, but he wouldn't even stay still long enough for me to confirm what he was hitting me with.

Every time I turned around to find him, I could see how Gabriel was doing fending off his five attackers. I watched the number drop to four, then three… He was down to the two talkative ones when one of the men on the ground got up and came at him from behind. Gabriel was concentrated on the front with only a knife in his hand, leaving him nothing to throw. I ignored my fight and blasted the guy away from him.

If Gabriel hadn't noticed the man before, he definitely reacted to him being thrown into the garbage can beside him. I wasn't even thinking about my bat-toting disappearing act when he popped in out of nowhere and gave me his best whack yet, right in the stomach.

I doubled over and fell to my knees, catching the anger in Gabriel's eye just as he threw his knife into my attacker, who'd had his arms raised to incapacitate me more permanently now that I was down. This left Gabriel weaponless with two Gifted ready to take their shots.

I forced myself to move past the fact that I was winded, and tried to blast the woman into the wall, since she was closest to him. Just as I shot my arms up, Gabriel reached for something sharp on the ground and stabbed her with it. I shifted to the guy coming at Gabriel from his right. He made a noise when he hit the wall, before falling to the ground.

I knew Gabriel would yell at me for my carelessness, his standard response to nearly losing me, but he was silenced by an elderly man who came out of nowhere, holding a box.

"Come," he said, opening a door to the building behind Gabriel.

"Who are you?" I asked, sensing that he was not a part of Henry's army. He felt... ethereal. Like he was a lot older than he looked.

"My family took care of the Bearers of the Crescent Moon for centuries. You need to get on the boat." He held the door open behind him, but kept walking.

"How do you know—"

"I know lots of things, Gabriel. I know that coronet won't help you if you get arrested, and I know that you are missing generations of Bearers from your line," he said while walking, not looking back once.

"How do we find them?" I asked, but Gabriel looked skeptical. Nell's book implied we were only missing one object, not generations worth.

"This is all you need." He lifted the box above his head, but held on to it as he brought us through corridors. "Kiki entrusted me with it before she…" he cut himself off and slowed the pace for a tiny moment. "It contains something from every Bearer that came before her."

He was like a human Rafiki, bringing us through an underground maze with no ending, but I could almost taste the salty air before he opened a door I hadn't seen in the pitch-dark hallway. The sun nearly blinded me as we stepped onto the top deck of the ship. Embry was below at the ticket counter, searching for us.

"How did you do that?" I asked the man.

"Remember where you came from, Lucy. Not just the pieces, but the whole picture." He put his hand on my sternum. My first instinct was to pull back, but his touch made my headache go away. It was warm and full of light, not that I understood his words.

He put the box in my hands, then bowed. When he stood up straight, he got this smile on his face, like he had accomplished something he'd been working on for a long time. Then he faded away. I don't know how else to describe it, except one second he was standing in front of me, and the next he was blowing into the wind.

"Wait!" I tried, but he was already gone.

Gabriel, who kept his head in all situations, went to the edge and called out to Embry, who was walking off in search of us and would have missed the ship.

"What was he?" I asked Gabriel before noticing that as shocked as he was, anger was his dominant emotion. And it was directed at me.

"You nearly died," he pointed out.

"What?" I was more focused on the guy with secret doorways

onto ships who disintegrated in front of us than on what happened in the alley.

"You put your own life at risk to save mine." He was fuming, trying to hold it in so he wouldn't yell at me and cause a scene, but also talking fast so Embry wouldn't witness it.

"He was going to kill you," I argued.

"It doesn't matter, Lucy. I don't matter."

"You matter to me." I took a step towards him, but the look in his eyes stopped me dead. Hatred and disgust were reflected back at me.

"This is another reason I shouldn't..." he cut himself off, shaking his head. "I'm Gifted. So if he had killed me, I would come back. And even if that wasn't the case, I am here to protect you. I meant it when I said I can't lose you Lucy, and it isn't just because of the prophecy, your birthmark, or a promise I made centuries ago." For a moment, his anger deflated, and I thought this was one of those times where he was yelling at me because he was scared, but he would realize that we were both okay now, and clearly stronger together. Instead, his eyes went cold as he said, "This was a mistake."

"Coming here, or..." I knew what he meant. A part of me had been expecting it from the very beginning, but hearing him say it... I couldn't breathe.

"I never should have kissed you. I'm sorry. It was my mistake to lead you on and... let's just go back to not talking." He wouldn't meet my eye as he went over to find Embry and tell him what happened. I felt like I'd been whacked in the stomach with a baseball bat all over again, only this time I couldn't catch my breath. I felt the warm tears welling up and roughly wiped them away. I didn't want to give him the satisfaction of seeing it, but he was breaking my heart.

. . .

PEOPLE WERE CROWDING onto the top deck, so I put the box in my backpack and watched the island disappear. I held onto the steel railing, bracing myself for a couple of hours of seasickness, but as I stared off into the distance with my heart breaking, I got flashes of someone else going through the same thing...

I knew I was Judith from the shawl I was wearing, the same one from her portrait at Alaric's estate. It was a different island that she was staring at, thinking of all the reasons why she was leaving, reminding herself of all the excuses why she shouldn't, but she still closed her eyes and looked inside her mind, into her own memories...

"Oh, Judith, you have perfect timing, my son should be here any minute," a woman said excitedly. She had ebony hair that was going gray, and I would guess her to be the owner of the apothecary-like shop Judith just walked into. It was more established than Nell's, but nothing compared to Ingrid's.

"Darling, come, I want you to meet a friend of mine," I heard while browsing through different herbs and roots.

"Mother, I don't have time for this."

I froze and felt a shiver run through me when I heard his voice, but Judith had an entirely different thought when she recognized him.

"Henry." His mother sounded stern, but he laughed at her.

"Fine, I'll say hello, but I have somewhere to be." He bent down to kiss her cheek.

The nearness of him paralyzed me with fear, but Judith was nervous with excitement, her heart reacting to him the way mine did to Gabriel.

"Henry, are you ready?" a female voice called from the doorway.

"Coming!" he responded. "I promise I'll meet your friend another time," he told his mother. "Nice to meet you," he called out through the shop on his way to the door.

"Oh, that boy... he drives me crazy sometimes." His mother shook her head in the direction he took while Judith walked over to her.

"Boys can be oblivious sometimes." Judith shrugged as the woman went to put the shop sign to 'closed', then ushered her to a back room.

"He will wake up one day and realize there is more to life than

parties and loose women, but until that happens..." She let out a deep breath, then took out a book. "Where were we?" I looked at the pages and recognized them as spells, before the memory changed...

I was sitting at the very back of a classroom, trying to be invisible in the all-male university. Henry sat in the row in front of me, occasionally turning back to talk to the person beside me. He was quick to put his coat on and head out as soon as class let out, so I hurried to bundle myself up and followed him.

"Henry!" I called, catching up to him on the stairs outside.

"Do I know you?" he asked.

"I'm Judith. Ric's friend. I sat behind you in class."

"Oh, of course." He was friendly and charming, like in Annabelle's first memory of him.

"I heard you asking about cosines. If you'd like, we could study together before the exam. My father was a professor, so..."

"You've been doing this for years," he understood.

"I'm studying on Saturday either way, so if you wanted to stop by, we could go through things. I'm sure you understand tangents way better than I do."

"Oh, I doubt that, but a study partner sounds nice. Judith, right?"

"Yes." I could feel her cheeks were on fire, though it probably looked like they were red from the cold, not from finally talking to him one on one...

All of a sudden, I was waiting at her home for someone who was never showing up, wearing something I would be more likely to wear to a ball than to a study session. I heard the door and felt her excitement bursting as she ran over, then took a moment to compose herself before opening it.

"Alaric," she said, confused.

"May I come in?" he asked. "It's freezing out here."

"I thought you were at the early Christmas party," she asked, stepping aside so he could warm himself up by the fire.

"I was, but then it got boring."

"Is boring code for Henry showed up?"

"For what it's worth, I think he had every intention of coming here before Anya showed up at his place."

"Not much." Judith took the pins out of her hair.

"I know you think you know him, and he was perfect that night, but the way he's treated you since..."

"I know," she assured her oldest friend, but I could feel her pain and reluctance. "I would have forgotten him and moved on, but he keeps showing up all over the place. I mean, what are the odds he would be in the only mathematics class they allowed me to attend?"

"What about Mrs. Hathorne's son? She thinks he's perfect for you," he reminded Judith, but she just looked at him over the bridge of her nose.

"He's Henry Hathorne. I heard his voice and nearly died," she admitted.

"What are you going to do?"

"Ace the exam, graduate top of the class, find my happily ever after." She shrugged, pretending she wasn't heartbroken, but the smile she gave him was genuine.

"You're amazing, Jude," he said, and I could tell how much he loved her, though I don't think she saw it. Yet.

"You're the only one who thinks so, but I plan on changing that." She didn't let it bring her down...

CHAPTER TWENTY-THREE

Once we got to the mainland, we immediately headed for the airport, where a man in a suit was waiting to bring us through a private security checkpoint. He then brought us to a small waiting room with half a dozen chairs, all spaced out in groups of two. I didn't think I could handle sitting next to Gabriel or having to answer Embry's questions about it. They were both acting like nothing happened, or that they didn't notice that something was off, but I could tell Embry knew. And more than once I caught Gabriel looking at me in a way that I had to bite my bottom lip to keep from reacting.

We each ended up taking a seat with an empty one beside us. I felt Embry itching to say something, so I took out the box the old man handed me. I still wasn't sure what happened to him. My best guess was that he was Gifted, waiting to give the box to a Bearer before he could move on, but no one said anything about them turning into sand once their task was done.

The box was old, probably red once upon a time, but it was now a faded pink. I lifted the cover and saw nothing but white tulle with what looked like pearls. I reached for one to see if it was attached, but wasn't surprised when I was pulled away...

I was Talina, surrounded by a group of women who were weaving the veil into my hair with pearls. They used large needles, with my hair as their thread, each woman placing a single pearl, adding to the ones that were already a part of the veil.

"Why are there so many people?" A little girl asked, holding tight to her pearl.

"It's a mother's love," Talina's mother, Xiomara, said in the voice my Grams used when she was telling me a story.

"But Talina only has one mother," the girl argued.

"My mother died years before I got married," Xiomara pointed out.

"No one was there?" The girl looked like she was about to cry.

"On the contrary. This ritual isn't meant to make the bride feel loss, but to show her that a mother's love comes in many shapes, sizes, and colors. My aunts all came together to put in my pearls, then my father took over at the end with my mother's pearl, as he had taken over after my mother passed."

"How many pearls are there?"

"One for every woman that came before Talina, for as long as time can tell." Xiomara winked at her, before some women left, letting others take their place.

The newcomers helped Talina slip into the dress that looked like it had also been passed down throughout the generations.

"You used to ask me if you could wear the beautiful dress every time there was a grand occasion." Xiomara had tears in her eyes as she smiled at her daughter in the gown.

"You always told me it was for weddings, nothing more," Talina remembered.

"And now it is yours, to give to your daughter, and her daughter after that."

The sun was setting by the time a new woman came, that I soon understood was Zeke's mother. "Not all daughters are made," she said, coming to stand behind me. "Some are found, to be received as a gift. You are mine." She put a delicate necklace around my neck.

I thought it was sweet of her, but Talina was so touched she cried...

· · ·

"WE HAVE ALL the ingredients for the Cure," I told Embry and Gabriel's expectant looks when I woke up. "This has pearls woven into it from every woman in Talina's line who came before her."

"I've reached out about the Arms of Yggdrasil, but so far everyone agrees that it doesn't exist, and if it does, they have no idea where to find it," Embry shared, having apparently done more research than just checking the museum for security cameras.

"Maybe there's only one," I suggested. "A family heirloom or guarded secret that wasn't advertised so it wouldn't be stolen. I mean, who even knows if any of the remnants of the True Cross are actually from the True Cross."

"But Henry already has everything he needs for the Coalescence, other than your heart." Gabriel went through our options, the vein in his forehead pulsing like it often did when he was mad or concentrating very hard on something.

"We can keep looking for it while running from him and his people every time they find us…"

"Or we can bring the fight to him and use his ingredients," Gabriel finished for me, then looked away when our eyes met.

"We don't have enough magic. There's no way we can win against him," Embry argued.

"If we distract him long enough, I can try to complete the ritual. That should give us more than enough power," I suggested.

"We'll figure something out," Gabriel decided, still not on board with anyone completing the ritual, given the essential ingredient of my heart.

While Gabriel went off to make calls or send codes or whatever it was he did, Embry came and sat beside me.

"What happened?" he asked, wrapping his arm around me.

"I opened the box and had a memory." It was pretty self-explanatory.

"I meant between you and Gabriel."

"Nothing happened," I lied, swallowing when he looked at me with disbelief.

"You couldn't take your eyes off each other last night, and now you're avoiding even glancing at one another," he pointed out.

"You're using your—"

"I don't purposely use it on either of you," he cut me off. "I actively try not to, but I know you, Luce, and your feelings are practically screaming at me."

"I'll try to be quieter."

"I can see your heart breaking, Tesoro." He looked to me like he could feel it as well.

"I'm just being silly. It's really the last thing that should be on our minds right now."

"It's not good for anyone if you're distracted," he warned.

"I got hurt. Not bad, but I took a blow to the stomach because he didn't see someone coming at him from behind," I came clean. I didn't feel like I had anything to be ashamed about.

"It distracted you," he understood.

"No, I miscalculated how long it would take me to blast the person coming at him before the person I was dealing with could reappear. He had this annoying disappearing act going on."

"Which had nothing to do with Gabriel being in danger."

"It had everything to do with him being in danger, but I wouldn't have done anything different if it was you in that alley or Ingrid or Sam or anyone. I was okay, but he wasn't, so I helped. And it was a baseball bat. No one was going to kill me."

"But Gabriel…."

"Completely overreacted and told me I was a mistake."

"You?" he seemed confused.

"You know what I mean," I reproached. Gabriel being upset with me and pushing me away because of his stupid overprotectiveness was something I could vent to Embry about. It was the same behavior he'd had at the plantation, only slightly magnified.

Last night, however, was not something I wanted to share with anyone except for Gabriel. Not that he would let me get anywhere near that topic now. "One step forward, twenty steps back." I shook my head.

"Sometimes people react emotionally instead of rationally."

"Three centuries of life experience does nothing to prevent immaturity?"

"When you've lost a lot of people, some of them to tiny moments of distraction, you don't use reason anymore, you react out of fear, doing whatever you can to keep the people you love safe, and make sure you don't lose anyone else. Especially when you look like someone he has watched die repeatedly." He pulled me close.

"Way to make me feel worse." I sighed.

"I don't want you to feel bad, love, I just thought you might want to understand."

"I'm never not going to be in danger, or not look like a woman he's lost a bunch of times."

"I disagree with the first one, and I think he just needs to figure out that it's better to be with the woman you love than to watch her love you from afar. Because it's not like either of you is safer pretending. It's the feelings that get you in trouble, not owning up to them." He was talking about him and Beth as much as me and Gabriel.

I took a deep breath and gave him what I hoped was a reassuring smile before doing my best to zip up my backpack with the veil's box inside. I removed a few things to reorganize it and accidentally dropped a loose sheet of paper. I opened the Chronicles to have a safer place to store it than letting it get all crumpled, then gasped when I picked it up. It was the landscape Gabriel had drawn on the boat to the island, only the scenery wasn't the focus. I completely understood why the two women were confused, because I was holding a drawing of myself. I was staring out into the distance with a smile and the tiniest of dimples. My hair was up in a messy bun with wisps falling and framing my face. It's not like I had always wanted him to draw me, but seeing that he had, even before we set foot on the island of cursed hope…

"I got us a ride to Salem." Gabriel came back and interrupted my thoughts. I quickly closed the Chronicles on his drawing as he handed us each a boarding pass.

"Are you sure about this?" Embry asked me.

"They keep finding us and if we do nothing, one of his men or these memories will do damage we can't come back from," I pointed out. "And this week is the crescent moon," I reminded him.

"Another FBI contact?" I asked Embry when we walked across the tarmac to a private jet. He was shaking his head and laughing to himself, but I didn't see what was so funny.

"This plane belongs to Angela's husband," he explained of Terrence's daughter, who was married to a pilot.

"Does he hate you as much as his wife does?" I smiled at the memory of how much Angela disliked Embry for turning her down when she threw herself at him in her youth.

"If he does, he hides it a lot better than she does." He winked before going up the stairs.

I wasn't sure if I was expecting it to be empty or to have celebrities on it, but I definitely wasn't expecting the group that greeted me once I boarded the flight.

CHAPTER TWENTY-FOUR

"What's going on?" I asked, turning back to face Gabriel, since he made our travel arrangements.

"If we're fighting to win, not just to survive, then we need a fighting chance," he said simply.

"We heard you could use a hand." Delia smiled at the shock on my face. I saw Tristan and Benjamin behind her, sitting at a table with a guy I didn't recognize. He hadn't looked up when I came in.

To their left was Caleb, looking unscathed from the flames I watched engulf his island safe house. I assumed the raven-haired bombshell on the couch with him was Etta, but when she looked up at me, struggling not to react as if I were Cassie, I also recognized her.

"Being a badass suits you," Caleb told me with a smile before I could say anything.

"I'm glad you're okay." I returned it.

"It'll take more than that to get rid of me, but they keep trying. This is my better half," he introduced.

"Etta." She extended her hand for me to shake, a firm grip where I had been expecting warmth.

"I saw you in a memory..." I tried to find a delicate way to tell her I saw a few moments of the night she died. It would have been better if I hadn't said anything at all. "I saw the night Cassie met you." I swallowed, figuring it got the point across without bringing it up.

"I'm surprised you recognized me." She exchanged a look with Gabriel before Caleb pulled her closer. I definitely wasn't on her good side so far.

"Your eyes," I said simply. "They left a mark."

"Not one of my finer moments. But a defining one for her." Etta looked deep into my eyes, then moved from my moonstone necklace down to my running shoes, sizing me up.

"I hope I can live up to her." I twisted the ring Clara gave me around my finger. Etta was nothing like how Caleb said she would treat me. Either because I'm not really Cassie, or because I was the cause of the fire on the island that claimed another one of Caleb's lives.

"Try to win," the guy from Tristan and Benjamin's table spoke up.

"I'll try my best," I told him, but he was getting looks from nearly everyone else.

"I'm just saying, Cassie went out in the middle of the night to confront him on her own and sacrificed herself to fix her mistake. I don't want to risk my life if this one will give up the minute it gets dangerous," he defended himself. He looked younger than me, with dark brown eyes and copper hair that looked like it was on fire when the sun reflected it.

I could see the vein pulsing in Gabriel's forehead as he clenched his fist, resisting the urge to punch him. To be honest, I didn't blame the guy for saying what everyone else was probably thinking.

"Is everyone ready?" the flight attendant came over and asked Gabriel, interrupting the stare-down, though I'm not sure the stranger was aware, or would have cared.

"We're good," he agreed.

"Then if everyone could please take their seats, I'll tell the captain we're ready for takeoff." She gave an awkward smile before shutting the door and going into the cockpit.

"Collin makes earthquakes, but he can't control the Gift and his emotions at the same time, so he often comes off a bit…"

"Like an asshole," Collin finished for Embry, who was trying to find a nicer way to describe his personality.

"This is a suicide mission," I told him bluntly. "I'm not going in blind like Cassie, because I know what he wants, and I know we don't stand a chance. But I'm still willing to try, and like Cassie, if it comes down to it, I would rather stab something through my own heart than let him win." I felt the dagger in my chest from when Kiara did just that and winced, feeling like a naïve child now that so many people were risking their lives for me.

"Let's go sit," Embry encouraged, gently nudging me. He brought me past everyone so we could take our seats in the back, while Gabriel stayed in the front with Delia.

"Do we have a plan?" I asked him, buckling my seat belt.

"We will go to the house Henry and Annabelle once shared and hopefully find Henry minimally surrounded. We will keep them busy while you get the missing ingredients for the ritual, and then we all live happily ever after." He gave me a smile, knowing that sounded more like a fairytale.

"Your plan lacks a lot of specificity," I warned.

"It depends how many henchmen he has, and what their skills are." He shrugged, but I was not happy with his nonchalance. "Most of us have been fighting together for centuries. We know each other's skills and weaknesses and know how to work together, even without a plan."

"And you'll let me venture off on my own while you fight a guy whose magic is stronger than anyone we've ever encountered?" I was both skeptical that they would let me out of their sight, into the lion's den, and not sure I wanted to leave them alone and magically defenseless.

"You'll never be alone," he said, like there was no other option. "And you're right, he is stronger than anyone we've encountered, but we know a lot of people who are strong on their own, so if we put them together…"

"I'm getting the feeling we will lose a lot of people."

"Luckily we all come back," he said in a way that told me I shouldn't worry, but he did me the courtesy of not using his Gift on me, and the words didn't do the trick.

"Even Collin?" I tried to lighten the mood.

"He gets better once his sister is around," he assured me.

"Can't you just… calm him down?" I suggested.

"He let me do it once when he was having a meltdown, but I tried to be helpful another time and nearly lost a life because of it."

"I guess no one likes to be manipulated," I ventured. "Were they just hiding out in Spain, waiting for us?"

"They were in France, about to head back to the States, so Gabriel got them to take a minor detour and change their destination."

"That's a big ask," I said the plan that would probably cost them their lives.

"We have this thing where if someone asks you for help, you go without questions."

"Because these are your best friends, or all Gifted?"

"More like family than best friends. We've all helped each other out so many times I don't think anyone knows who owes who anymore. I could gladly go a century without seeing Collin, but if he was in trouble, I would go to him. Without a second thought."

"It's nice that you have that." I looked around the plane. It was nice that it wouldn't just be the three of us, but we were nowhere near enough to defeat Henry. I couldn't even sense a trace of magic from any of them.

"More are coming," Embry assured me. I tried to hide how

relieved I was, but we needed a lot more people. "The connection in Mexico was not an accident, and I'm sure some will meet us in Salem."

"He knows we're coming, doesn't he?" I asked, but the question was rhetorical. Henry told Donovan his plan was to sit back and wait for me to come to him, and although he hadn't barged his way into my mind since the forest, I got the feeling these headaches were supernatural.

We'd barely been in the air for an hour when we hit a patch of turbulence. I instinctively reached out for Embry's hand, and he gave me a reassuring smile that showed me why he got his particular Gift. It amplified his natural abilities.

"Good evening, ladies and gentlemen, this is your Captain speaking. We're experiencing some slight turbulence, but I am told it should clear up momentarily as we make our descent. Please get back to your seats and we'll be landing shortly."

"We're nowhere near Mexico," I told Embry.

"I guess we're bringing Kate." He gave me a knowing smile, but I had no idea who Kate was.

It was getting dark, but I could still make out the landscape from my window. We were approaching an island, probably the same size as the Island of the Enchanted Moon, but all I saw was grass, trees, a river, and log cabins. As we got closer, I felt nearly Donovan-level magic.

"Is Kate…"

"A witch?" he asked as the turbulence stopped suddenly, replace by what I can only describe as a tugging feeling, before the plane went silent. I had wondered how we would land without a runway, but I was not expecting this.

I knew we landed because I could see how close we were to the ground, but I didn't feel a thing.

"Sorry 'bout that, Mallory doesn't like visitors." A girl with flaming red hair came in through the side door of the plane, that opened seemingly of its own accord.

"Collin's sister?" I whispered to Embry.

"Jazmin," he agreed. "You'll like her."

She was followed by five women and two men, but only one of them caught my eye. Her pink hair didn't help, but it was the way she looked at me, like she wanted to run over and give me a hug.

They had two bags between the eight of them, and the same resigned look. Within minutes of our landing, a girl with blonde hair closed her eyes and made the entire plane rise into sky, slowly getting higher and higher, until the engines kicked in and we were flying again.

"THE ONE WITH the silver hair is Kate. She tired of hiding her magic and her Gift, so she started a commune on the island with her sister and a few friends. I think they're twenty of them now, but they don't live there all the time, and most of them don't owe us anything," Embry explained before leaning back in his chair. I think the goal was just to rest his eyes, but within minutes he was asleep, his soft breathing occasionally interrupted by a snore.

I took out the Book of Shadows and went through the pages, trying to find something that could help us with what we were about to attempt. I found nothing even remotely useful against Henry, so I sighed and leaned into the aisle, trying to sneak a look at Gabriel. On the off-chance that he was awake while everyone around him slept, I could maybe go over and...

"There's something about his intense broodiness that makes my knees buckle too," the girl with the pink hair interrupted my plans as she came and sat beside me. "I'm Jen."

"Lucy," I told her. "I was just stretching." It was none of her business, but I felt the need to defend myself.

"We all know who you are." She rolled her eyes at me. "It's cute that you introduce yourself. Although I guess Rosenberg calls you the new Cassie, but even he knows your real name."

"Is he here too?" I asked, looking around. There were still a few more people I didn't know, but Rosenberg was a name I remembered. Caleb had described him as someone who likes confrontation, in a way that made me feel like I never wanted to meet him. Although I guess beggars can't be choosers.

"He's meeting us there. Which is good, because he doesn't like plane rides, and no one enjoys being near him when he's not happy."

"But he's on our side?" I had to make sure.

"He likes to fight, but it's not like he goes around beating people up or insulting guys at bars to start them. I wouldn't want to spend more time with him than I have to, but if I was in trouble, he would have my back," she assured me. I guess they all were like family, where even if you don't like each other, you're still there for them.

"You both knew Cass?"

"I think he fought with her at some point. She was always running around saving people." She smiled, but it wasn't the way she looked at me when she walked in.

"Eugenia here is way more ancient than that," one of the guys from the commune joined our conversation.

"How ancient?" I asked, regretting my decision to use his wording instead of putting it more delicately. They might be close enough to tease each other, but I wasn't.

"Annie was the one I saw when I walked in," she answered the question I'd been trying to ask.

"That would mean you knew Embry and Gabriel." I turned to Embry, but he was fast asleep beside me.

"I told you he made my knees buckle." She looked over to Gabriel and gave me a knowing smile.

"Who makes your knees buckle?" the guy asked.

"He made. You make," she assured him with a kiss.

"I'm Peter." He extended his hand once they pulled apart.

"Lucy." I shrugged apologetically, but I wasn't just going to assume everyone in the world knew my name. "What about Henry?" I pressed, going back a few questions.

"I died in a very obvious way, so when I woke up, I knew I couldn't just go back to my old life. I did the whole sit in the back pew and listen to my own funeral, then I left town and never came back. I eventually ended up with Delia and was pleasantly surprised when Gabriel showed up for Christmas one year."

Peter introduced me to Lara and Gigi, both of whom had magic in addition to their Gifts, but I mostly sat back and listened to them tease each other and hang out like we weren't about to face my worst nightmare.

"You should get some sleep, Lucy. There won't be much rest once we get there," Jen told me before everyone found themselves a corner and they turned off the lights.

I didn't think I would ever get to sleep with what I knew was waiting for us once we got to Salem, but the roller coaster of emotions from the past few days and my lack of sleep eventually caught up to me.

I WOKE up as a half-dozen newcomers were boarding the plane, which told me we were in Mexico. My sights immediately landed on Terrence, who was being led by a man with dreadlocks. I wouldn't have been concerned, only he was blindfolded and wearing noise-cancelling headphones. Once he was sitting, he took out needles and started knitting what looked like a poncho.

"Is he okay?" I asked Embry, who looked about as alert as I was.

"Terrence will be with us once we get to Salem, but we thought it was best to not let them in on all of our plans," he explained, reminding me that Terrence had been touched by a Gifted who now had access to his mind. He couldn't control it, but he could report whatever he saw inside.

I wanted to check out the new arrivals, but they turned the lights out again and everyone seemed to be sleeping. Except for Gabriel, whose eyes found mine in the dark before he looked away, crushing me. I panicked slightly over the fact that our next stop was Salem, where Henry was waiting, but at some point between the hyperventilating and attempts to calm down, I fell asleep.

We landed at a private airport that looked more like a paved backyard than an actual runway and were greeted by at least ten cars. One driver looked miserable, with his hands permanently balled into fists, so I assumed he was Rosenberg.

I spotted Ingrid, looking like her grown-up illusion, and was rushing over to make sure she was okay when I saw, "Sam!"

"Don't sound so happy to see me," he reproached, taking me into his arms.

"This is the dangerous stuff you're not supposed to be a part of," I explained.

"You're not either." He kissed the top of my head, then let me take Ingrid in for a hug. I tried to give him a look like we would talk about this after, but he didn't seem the least bit concerned.

"It's good to see you," Ingrid told me once we pulled apart.

There was a sense of excitement and fear in the air. It was what I imagined sports teams felt before they went out on the field, but then again, most athletes didn't die if they lost their games.

Watching them come up with our strategy, I realized it was much more like troops preparing for a battle. Gabriel, Embry,

Kate, Delia, and Rosenberg all huddled together around a map they made on the ground from rocks and sticks, saying things like, "The witches will hang back as long as they can," and "We can use the muscle for that." The only mystery element was me.

"What do we do with her?" Rosenberg moved his head to the side in my general direction.

"She'll come with us," Embry decided.

"It'll be game over before half of us show up," Rosenberg argued.

"With Sam?" Delia asked Gabriel. I wasn't thrilled by how in sync they seemed to be, but she was a lot like me. She sat back and listened to everyone, but when she spoke, it was usually whatever I was thinking, right before I could cut in to say it. And people listened.

"Embry and I will drive together while Sam hides Lucy. I need everyone to stay back as far as possible until we're at the door. Once the fighting starts and everyone is outside, Sam and Lucy will go inside and find the missing ingredients. As soon as they have them, Sam will send up a flare and we get the hell out of there." Gabriel looked around and got nods of agreement from everyone.

"Let's get the party started." Rosenberg clapped his hands, making more than a few of us jump, before everyone headed for a car, and we left.

By the time Embry finally pulled into a driveway, I knew we were in the right place. Even without the garden that I recognized from Annabelle's memories… there was just something dark and ominous about the house. It looked like all the other ones from the outside, but I could feel it.

I could see the gazebo in the distance, but it was in a state of disrepair, like no one had bothered with it since Annabelle left. The fields surrounding it looked like they were left to their own devices except for a tiny patch right beside the house that was in full bloom.

"It's not too late to change your mind," Embry tried, looking to me and Sam in the back seat. The only part of the plan I wanted to change was me hiding inside while everyone else engaged in battle outside.

"I made up my mind months ago," I assured him.

I was even more sure Henry knew we were here. He was always a million steps ahead of us, and even I could sense all the magic back at the airport. We were hoping mine would be lost in the sea of other powers. Or maybe our magic didn't come anywhere near to even comparing to him, and we were thus less than blips on his radar.

Gabriel opened the back door to take his weapon, but his eyes rested on me. I bit my bottom lip and looked up at him, trying to convey everything I knew I couldn't say to him, especially before a fight. That he needed to be careful, that I loved him, that I didn't think we were a mistake, and I couldn't lose him. His eyes tried to be cold and professional, like when he was trying to run from his feelings at the beginning of the summer, but I could tell he also wanted to reach out and pull me close, so I could be safe in his arms. He lifted his hand, but Sam took my arm before he could do anything. We both needed to be invisible to get out of the SUV unnoticed.

Henry opened the door as the guys stepped onto the porch, wearing dress pants and a button-down shirt. This normalcy somehow made him even scarier. He took his time to walk out and join them, while his men stayed huddled behind him. I counted five, but there were probably more waiting inside.

"Can I help you?" Henry asked with that twisted smile, looking behind them, searching for me. I trusted Sam's Gift, but I still pulled him behind the SUV. It was bad enough that everyone in a ten-mile radius could hear my heart racing.

"We came for the spell," Embry said. "The one that keeps her alive."

"You did?" Henry looked amused. "And what gave you the impression that I would give you the spell?" he asked. "Or do you plan on making a trade?"

"No, we plan on taking the spell and keeping her alive," Gabriel said.

Henry tried to read their faces. They wouldn't have shown up blind and unprepared, hoping for a miracle after centuries of running from him at all costs. He started laughing as if Gabriel had just told him the most hilarious joke he'd ever heard, before he stopped, as suddenly as he had started.

I knew he'd already sensed them, like I had, but our reinforcements were coming into Henry's view. He looked more annoyed than worried, but I knew we had a sizeable enough group to at least give him pause. He snapped his fingers and without a word, the men who had been waiting behind filed past him to fight Gabriel and Embry, who were closest.

Henry had a few more lackeys who materialized out of nowhere, but they were incredibly outnumbered. Not that it mattered much when we had Terrence, whose Gift was taking confessions, fighting against a woman whose arms turned into tentacles that allowed her to choke four people at once.

Most of the Gifts on our side were rather harmless, or at least defensive, while Henry's men were groomed to kill. Still, those with the most passive powers seemed to have trained harder to compensate. Sure, the way Rosenberg made his arms turn into swords, spiked balls, and carving knives at will was terrifying, but Etta wielding her whip looked deadly. Everyone was holding their own, except for Ingrid, Kate, Lara, Gigi, and the man with the dreadlocks, who were fighting Henry, hands clasped together to pool their powers. Even from where I stood behind the car, I could feel how strong their combined powers were, but it was nothing compared to Henry's. Even the metal spikes Mallory kept shooting at Henry whenever she had the chance weren't doing much damage. Unless I got the missing ingredients soon, they would not last long. I could only imagine what would happen to everyone else if Henry was no longer distracted.

I couldn't see myself, or Sam, but he followed without question when I brought us towards the house. Henry looked distracted enough to not notice, but a part of me was convinced he could still see us, or at least sense me.

THE HOUSE LOOKED like it belonged in a photoshoot for a magazine, not like anyone lived in it. Everything was meticulously laid out to achieve the perfect look, except for the dining room that had leftover coffee cups and fast food bags all over it. I wondered if Henry had a rotating group of guards at all times, or if he brought his army here around the time he started actively hunting me.

"What are we looking for exactly?" Sam asked in a whisper once we were in what I assumed was Henry's office.

"Splinter's from the cross Jesus was crucified on, vervain, a wooden cup, and my heart," I shared, looking for a safe rather than items lying around.

"I found the last one." I could hear the smile in his voice, but he was keeping a hand on me to keep me invisible, even while everyone else was outside.

"This will take forever if you hold on to me," I warned.

"It'll take even longer if you're dead."

"We closed the door, and I can sense when his magic is close," I pointed out.

We had a mini staring competition before he decided it was better to get me out of there faster than to keep me invisible while in a locked room, riffling through Henry's things.

Sam took the left side of the room while I scoured the right, which included a mahogany desk and three towering bookshelves. I gently pulled out each book, half-expecting the walls to shift and reveal a hidden passage to his secret lair.

"I found a safe," Sam whispered, pulling me from my menial task.

"Try 0108," I suggested.

"What's that?"

"The day he married Annabelle." If that didn't work, I would suggest Margaret's birthday, but my hopes weren't high on that one.

I didn't get to find out if I was right. I had barely touched the wooden chalice to move it aside, not even thinking of the cup of Yggdrasil, when I was gone…

"You're not supposed to see the bride on the wedding day." I was Talina, talking to the guy from the crowd of her coronation. His guilty smile immediately mollified her reproach.

"I asked to spend the rest of my life with you, not to spend twenty-four hours without being able to see you," he argued, standing up to wrap his arms around her.

"You make an excellent point." She buried her head into his chest. "Is everything ready?"

"My mother woke this morning with a fear that there won't be enough food," he shared.

"My father is helping her," Talina agreed.

"Are you sure that this is what you want?" He brought up the real reason he came. His concern made others doubt him, Talina knew that, but it was one of the main reasons she decided on the full ceremony, rather than the partial one the women in her family usually performed.

"If something matters to you, go all in," she repeated her mother's words.

"All I can offer is my love," he reminded her, like he was worried it wasn't enough.

"And the purest of hearts. The warmest of smiles. The smoothest tongue to calm the voices inside my head, the strongest arms to hold me when I need to feel safe... you are more than worthy my love," Talina said before giving Zeke a kiss, letting it go further than she'd intended before the ceremony, but she didn't want him to doubt himself.

"There are enough traditions being broken, I'll not let you break another," Talina's mother warned, coming in with a basket that held what looked like a wedding dress.

"And the first rule is to make sure I never upset you, Xiomara." He gave her a warm smile.

"Empty words, Zeke." She pretended to be stern, but her eyes smiled throughout.

"I shall see you both at dusk." He bowed before retreating, leaving Xiomara to give her daughter a look.

"He worries he is not worthy," Talina explained his presence to her mother.

"It won't work if he isn't," Xiomara said simply.

"You told me to marry for love." She was confused.

"You wouldn't love someone who wasn't worthy." Xiomara waved her daughter's comment away.

"Mama," she reproached.

"You can marry whoever you choose. The bonds of the flesh need only the vows, and even then..." Xiomara shrugged like vows were not entirely necessary for that kind of bond.

"Mama!" Talina reproached once more.

"The Coalescence will not happen if Zeke is not worthy. You choose with your heart, but being worthy of love, and being worthy of your burden are not the same thing."

"How will we know if it worked?"

"There will be no doubt in anyone's mind. The legend is that the Coalescence is so miraculous to behold that it bathes the world in light."

"Have you seen it before?"

"My grandfather used to say he chose not to steal my grandmother's glory, but it was because he would fall short," was her way of letting Talina know it had been generations since anyone saw it.

"Zeke is the best man I know. If he is not worthy, no man is," Talina shared. "I've always resented the idea that love makes you blind. I think it gives you a perfect understanding of another human being. I see every fault and every good deed, so I know what kind of man he is."

"Then I look forward to the brightest night in memory." Xiomara hugged her daughter before carefully removing items from her basket. "Are you ready to begin?"

"Yes mama." Talina smiled and took a deep breath.

The memory continued with the Mother's Love ceremony I saw at the airport, before Talina followed Zeke's mother outside and went to stand at the front of the crowd, where Zeke was waiting. He took my hands in his and brought me to an altar. The smile on my face couldn't express half the happiness Talina was feeling.

"You are the beat of my heart and the air in my lungs. You are the light in my life and the song in my soul," he started, the nerves seeming to calm when he looked into Talina's eyes, mirroring her tears.

"I take you for the love you hold in your heart, and the goodness in your soul."

"I vow to spend my life caring for you and being true."

"You are my priority, giving me strength through hard times and sharing my joy in good times."

"I promise you honesty and patience, to spend each day becoming a better version of myself, and helping you to do the same."

They took turns reciting the vows, before Zeke walked over to a table I hadn't noticed before. There was a wooden cup in the middle of it, and he took a candle to light it on fire.

"From the kindling of Emmanuel's Betrayal burns the soul of his untouched child," he said the familiar words with his hands hovering above the flames.

"Let the tears of Isis fuel the flames in the arms of Yggdrasil," he added a handful of vervain, then took a ceremonial dagger and sliced

into his own hand, "As the blood of the incumbent quells the fire, may the heart of the Bearer of the Crescent Moon originate the Coalescence."

Talina took the dagger and sliced into her own palm, so by the time Zeke said Coalescence, he pressed his cut hand into hers, locking their fingers together, before a light, brighter than any I have ever seen, burst from my heart and surrounded us all. Everyone except Zeke, who completely disappeared into the light…

I was breathing fast when I came back to myself, trying to process what I just saw. So many thoughts were going through my mind. Mostly the fact that those words weren't actually for a ritual to summon power through nefarious means, but also how my heart wasn't so much an ingredient as where the 'coalescence' bursts out from. Then again, the Coalescence looked more like a wedding than anything else.

I turned and excitedly told Sam what I saw, grateful this was one of the times where I acted out the memory rather than passing out. I saw Sam's face light up, but before he could reply, I got a sinking feeling in my stomach and turned to find Henry standing in the doorway.

"Do I even bother offering you the chance to join me, one last time?" he asked, stepping closer to me. I stepped back, but there was a wall behind me. I could no longer see Sam and hoped he was gone to get help rather than doing something reckless.

"I would still rather die," I told him.

Sam chose that moment to rush at Henry with a letter opener. He was invisible, so I saw the weapon disappear from the table a second before the flick of Henry's hand sent Sam flying into the wall.

"It seems a pity to knock out the last of my line, but if you leave me no other choice…" Henry said as if Sam was nothing more than a fly he'd swatted away.

"Go to hell," I said, resigned to not let him see my fear. The fact that no one followed him inside the house did not bode well for the men and women who came with me.

"Been there, done that," he said, his smile making my skin crawl before he put up his hand and I suddenly felt paralyzed, unable to move or even scream. It was just like Cassie's dreams, and it turned out my magic was useless too. "Now I promised you I would cut your heart out of your still beating chest, and I am sure you have figured out that I am a man who keeps his promises," Henry said with a gleam before pulling a knife out of nowhere and planting it in the top of my chest, far enough from my heart or any major arteries so he wouldn't damage the coveted ingredient, but also ensuring that I would be alive to feel the pain for as long as possible.

Inside, I was screaming. In agony, and for Gabriel and Embry, but I knew I wasn't making a sound, just like my arms and legs were refusing to move as I willed them to. I had just decided to do like Beth had done, to close my eyes and let death take me, but Henry wasn't done with me yet. He stood and stared at me for a moment that felt like an eternity before saying, "It wasn't really you I made that promise to. Your misfortune lies in that you look so incredibly like her. The birthmark is your actual curse, but my Annie, she broke a lot of hearts."

The knife was in my chest, but he was taking his absolute time killing me.

"You may not believe it, but I loved her once. More than life itself, I thought. I saw her crescent moon on our wedding night. Having it be on her neck nearly took all the joy out of it. I found the last piece of my puzzle, that I had spent over a century trying to complete, yet I couldn't bear to use it. I spent years searching for a way to achieve my life's purpose without losing her. There was a time I hoped that her loving me would be enough. My heart was hers, so if she loved me the same, I might have..." He stopped cutting, and looked away from me. When he came back to me, he was no longer nostalgic. If I didn't know any better, I would think he was hurt. "Unfortunately, she had taken my heart, but given hers to another. I should have killed her then, but still, she was the mother of my child, and I was convinced I could make her love me. I thought the spell in her grimoire solved all our problems, but she broke my heart all over." The anger in his voice was reflected in his movements, as the knife went farther than it had previously, catching my breath.

CHAPTER TWENTY-SIX

The thoughts were swirling in my head. Henry had me alone, Sam was knocked out, and I didn't know if some of the people outside were still fighting, or if everyone was dead. Either way, no one was coming to save me.

But, if the coalescence was a wedding, it seemed like the light came out of Talina's chest. As if the power Zeke gained wasn't summoned from the Gods, but came directly from inside her.

The blood loss must have been getting to me, because I kept seeing that dream, where I couldn't reach Sam on my own, so all of my ancestors came and helped me, then Dream Beth told me I already had everything I needed. If that wasn't just my imagination, then maybe the magic was already somewhere inside me, flowing through the blood of my ancestors, and I just needed to unlock it.

Everything for Kiara's Cure was in my bag in the car, but the guys insisted my magic was about intent, that I didn't need an object as long as I was strong enough to channel it on my own. Which they seemed to think I was.

Henry was still talking about Annabelle, but I closed my eyes and focused on each Bearer before me. I focused on the moments they shared with me. Cassie being shot and jumping off the cliff to save her daughter. Beth being burned alive. Rosie's heart breaking when Gabriel turned her down. Annabelle accidentally cutting herself to impress Gabriel. Judith waiting for a Henry who never showed up. Talina's joy on her wedding day… I focused on their emotions and pleaded for their help. I asked for the powers of my ancestors to defeat the man who took so much from so many of us…

It wasn't a burst of light so much as a ball of warmth that formed in my chest, radiating through my entire body. I could feel it building, filling me up, but it wasn't until Gabriel and Embry barged into the office that I realized I could move again.

HENRY TRIED to send them against the wall like he had Sam, but my hands shot up and Henry was knocked backwards instead, as if something bumped into his shoulder.

"I thought I made you stay put." Henry turned to face me, sending shivers down my spine. I could feel his magic trying to hold me in place as he turned back to the guys, but I fought back.

Embry and Gabriel both stood in front of me, putting a barrier between Henry and me.

"How cute. Ready for another round?" Henry asked, confident in the knowledge that they'd never won against him.

Embry took his sword and rushed at Henry, but he was thrown up in the air before he could get close. I saw Henry bring his hands down as if to smash Embry into the ground, so I put my hands out to slow his fall.

Gabriel looked to me, shocked by what I did – and by the dagger in my chest – but I was oddly calm. Henry wasn't panicking, so I must look normal, but every one of my nerve endings was firing with warmth and electricity.

"What did you do?" Henry asked me, his smile fading as he

realized I was no longer the weak teenager he was up against earlier.

"Asked for a little help." I put my hands in front of me, ready for him to throw something at me, but he looked like he was calculating his next move.

"I still have the True Cross, you can't have completed the ritual," he told me.

"The ritual only gives you access to what's already mine."

"I guess I'm a few cuts away from sharing it then," Henry said with a confidence I didn't buy.

"If you prove yourself worthy, which I don't think is likely," I argued.

"It's my birthright." He was getting angry, which made him look like a child.

"It was. A long time ago. But I think we both know you're not that boy anymore."

He looked at me like I was crazy before creating a great big ball of energy between his hands. His smile, though much less confident, was back. He rightfully guessed that although I was suddenly more powerful than him, he'd had centuries to figure out how to use his powers, and I barely had a summer.

I stood there and waited for Henry to strike, grateful that the guys each took a step back so I wouldn't have to worry about them getting caught in the crossfire. Henry split the great ball of energy into three smaller ones and shot them at me, one after another. I could deflect them with my force shield, which was clearly much stronger than it was when I threw Gabriel against the tree. Henry's power balls shot through the house and landed in the gazebo out back. I could only tell because the fire was visible from the window.

Eventually, Henry used his brain instead of his skills and shot his energy balls at the guys I would give my life for. I deflected all three, but wasn't quick enough to stop the one he shot at me right after. It caught me in the stomach, and I doubled over, the wind knocked out of me. I took a second to look at Henry with all the hatred I was feeling, then released a devastating gust of wind that knocked him off his feet.

Apparently, even without practice, my ancestors gave me the skills I needed to kick Henry's butt. We went back and forth with the powerful air strikes, before Henry switched to lightning. It was a horrible idea because anything he did, I could do so much better. Unlike the air, that seemed to be a temporary inconvenience, the lightning I shot sent Henry fifty feet into the air, before he landed with a horrible crunch of breaking bones.

"IF YOU KILL ME NOW, they die too," Henry warned as I walked over, about to strike him with more lightning.

I finally felt like I had the upper hand, but his words stopped me. His smile was gone, and he resorted to pleading for his life, but the words struck me to my core.

"Protecting you from me was the only thing keeping the two of them alive," he said, making me turn to Embry. He nodded as a goodbye, resigned to dying.

I knew their deaths were the most likely outcome after defeating Henry, but to be honest, I never thought we would get this far.

"As long as you can never hurt her again, I'm perfectly okay with that." Gabriel locked eyes with me, giving me permission to do what I needed to do.

I held on to that eye contact a few moments, then took a deep breath and released a laser-like energy that made Henry glow for a few seconds before the light turned into fire and he erupted into flames. It was a brilliant spectacle until all that remained was a pile of ash.

I stared at the pile and waited for Henry to come back, unable to believe it was really over. I wanted to ask Gabriel and Embry, but I wasn't ready to look over and find out if they'd drifted away like the old man on the boat.

I'd been ignoring the wound in my chest, but it hurt so much now that I wasn't fighting for my life. My bleeding had slowed while I was under Henry's control, but the fight exacerbated it. The blood loss was making me so woozy that I fell to the ground. Relief washed over me as the guys rushed over. My death was a reasonable price to pay for the world to be rid of Henry.

"Lucy!" Embry said frantically, lifting my head into his lap while trying to put pressure on my wound. "Gabriel went to get the Cure, you'll be okay," he assured me, but I felt myself drifting away, and knew they didn't have much time.

Gabriel came back into the room with the backpack and set everything up for Kiara's Cure. "It will be okay," he told me, but the fear I was starting to no longer feel was in every word he said.

They followed all the steps, the two of them becoming so blurry that I could hardly tell them apart. I could tell from the tone of their voices that it wasn't working, but they kept rereading the paper and trying again.

"It's okay," I told them.

"We are not letting you die, Lucy. We will find a way," Gabriel told me.

"Take my heart," I told him, having so much trouble swallowing.

"What?" he asked, visibly shocked.

"There," I said, lifting my arm so I could point to Embry's paper, which he figured out even though my hand dropped almost as soon as it went up.

"We can't…"

"Take my heart," I told Gabriel, as authoritative as I could manage under the circumstances.

"We need to complete the ritual." I heard the reluctance in Embry's voice.

"I can't…"

"Gabriel…" I said, pleading with my eyes because I couldn't find my words. I saw tears in his black eyes as he looked back at me, but I couldn't really keep mine open anymore.

"I love you," Gabriel whispered, or it seemed like he was whispering, because it came from so far away.

"We will bring you back," Embry promised me, though I could barely hear anything at that point.

I felt light as a feather, and warm when my eyes finally closed. I knew that unless they completed the ritual and the spell, my eyes would never open again. I thought it would terrify me, that I would be screaming about not being ready to die, but the warmer and lighter I felt, the less I worried about being too young or all the things I hadn't done.

CHAPTER TWENTY-SEVEN

When Lucy stopped breathing and they knew she was gone, Gabriel and Embry just sat there, watching her inert body. They were both used to death, and they had watched this woman die many times, but seeing it was always hard. It didn't help that Lucy was younger than the others. Too young. They couldn't process the scene in front of them.

It wasn't until Embry gently closed her eyelids that Gabriel found his voice. "What do we need to do?" he asked, the emotion making it raw.

They split the list in half and went around the property, as well as through their own bag, to find everything they needed to perform the ritual that would grant one of them the terrible power they needed to save her.

Most of the items from the list were scattered around Henry's office, his ego preventing him from properly hiding them. Vervain was one of the few plants still growing in the garden, but the True Cross proved to be a challenge.

"If he knew we didn't have it, it can't just be lying around somewhere. It would be in the safe or a secure location." Embry scanned the room for something they might have missed. The safe opened on Margaret's birthday, which was only the third combination they tried, but it only held passports, money, and paperwork.

"How could he know we didn't find it somewhere else? There are pieces of it all over." Gabriel tried to control his breathing, but the longer they left Lucy lying there, the less convinced he was that they could bring her back.

"Unless most of them are fake. If you added up all the fragments known as the True Cross, you could rebuild a dozen of them," Embry pointed out.

"If I had something like that, I would never let it out of my sight," Gabriel got the words out before a flash went off in his head. It was less of a flash and more of a panicked rush to the pile of ash that Henry had become. Sifting his hands through the cursed remnants, he quickly found what he was looking for; a tungsten vial.

"He put it inside himself." Embry swallowed hard.

"No one knew the cup existed, so he hid it in plain sight, but the coveted True Cross he kept with him at all times." Gabriel brought his hand to the scar from when Embry dug inside him to take out a similar object.

They brought everything back to Lucy and set it up, following the instructions down to the letter, with no room for mistakes.

"Are you ready to do this?" Embry asked once they got down to the final element, the one neither of them was ready to retrieve.

"No, but I'm not ready to lose her either," Gabriel said fiercely.

They turned to Lucy, with Embry holding the encrusted dagger they were supposed to use to cut out her heart. As soon as he got close enough to see her, to feel her skin that was growing cold, but still felt like she was there, he froze. She looked like she was playing her trick on them, pretending to sleep so you would carry her or talk to her or...

"I can't," Embry said, dropping the knife.

"The one who cuts out her heart is the one who gets the magic. It has to be you," Gabriel argued, not trusting himself with that kind of power. It wasn't something he coveted or was worried he would abuse, but Embry was way more inherently good than he was. The power probably wouldn't have any altering effects on him.

"Then it has to be you, Gabriel. I can't." Embry handed over the knife.

GABRIEL LOOKED at the dagger in his hand, then to Lucy, lying so peaceful in front of him, and couldn't reconcile the two. Couldn't accept what he had to do. You would have to be a heartless monster to cut into her, even if she was dead. He had to remind himself that this was the only way to save her, before he closed his eyes, mentally preparing himself to make the incision.

Gabriel opened his eyes and brought the dagger to Lucy's chest just as Sam woke up and rushed at him, crying "Stop!"

"Keep him back," Gabriel warned, taking a deep breath. It was hard enough to do this without someone begging him not to.

"The coalescence isn't a ritual to summon magic, it binds two people together so they can share the magic she already has," Sam explained what Lucy had told him earlier.

"But her heart…" Embry argued.

"Is not an ingredient. It's where the magic comes from. To complete the ritual, her heart needs to choose you."

"Her heart…"

"You don't need to cut it out of her chest because it's already yours," Embry understood, turning to his oldest friend.

"What do I do?" Gabriel was relieved he didn't need to cause more damage, but terrified they were wrong, that this wouldn't work.

"Read this and mean it," Embry said, handing him the paper

with Lucy and Annabelle's birthmark on it. Gabriel didn't have trouble meaning it, he didn't even have to pretend that he believed every word, because if this didn't work, then he had lost her.

"You are the beat of my heart and the air in my lungs. You are the light in my life and the song in my soul," he began, looking to Embry for confirmation before looking down at Lucy. This was a confession of love, not a summoning of power. "I take you for the love you hold in your heart, and the goodness in your soul. I vow to spend my life caring for you and being true. You are my priority, giving me strength through hard times and sharing my joy in good times. I promise you honesty and patience, to spend each day becoming a better version of myself, and helping you to do the same. From the kindling of Emmanuel's Betrayal burns the soul of his untouched child. Let the tears of Isis fuel the flames in the arms of Yggdrasil," Gabriel added the vervain, then took the dagger and used it to cut into his hand so his blood could pour into the cup. "As the blood of the incumbent quells the fire, may the heart of the Bearer of the Crescent Moon originate the Coalescence."

"I don't think it worked." Gabriel said once he recited all the words on the paper, thus completing the ritual. He'd expected it to wash over him, maybe see a flash of light or fireworks.

"It definitely worked," Embry assured him, as Lucy's chest glowed bright, before everything around them was bathed in light.

It seemed like Sam and Embry could no longer see or hear him, as they looked around, trying to find him.

"She said there was a test of worthiness," he heard Sam telling Embry.

That would have been good to know before they wasted their only chance of saving her on him.

. . .

GABRIEL WONDERED if he had to prove that Lucy was worthy of being saved, which would be easy, or that he was worthy of saving her, which would be much harder. He waited for the test, or instructions, but there were none. He checked to see if Lucy was waking up, but she was still on the ground a few feet away, not moving.

All of a sudden, Gabriel found himself in a white room he could only describe as soft. He looked around, wondering how he could prove their worthiness. Then he heard it.

"Gabriel," she said softly from behind him, but he knew that when he turned around, it would be Annabelle. All the girls' voices were the same. It wasn't even the accent that gave it away, but no one said his name the way she did.

"Belle." He turned around slowly, afraid she would disappear if he made any sudden movements. She was as beautiful as he remembered, her eyes looking at him like they always had, like she loved him more than anything in the world, and in her eyes, he could do no wrong.

"My love." She moved close and put her hand on his cheek, so he closed his eyes and relished it. He could die now and be happy, but thinking of dying reminded him of Lucy, who was counting on him to save her.

"I came here to save Lucy. She's dying and I need to bring her back," he explained. The woman in front of him had died centuries ago, but he believed in the afterlife, that Annabelle had been up there watching him all those years.

"You have the power to bring her back," Annabelle agreed in a way that told him there was a catch. "But you can only bring back one of us."

"What do you mean?" he asked, not sure he understood what she was suggesting.

"You can bring back whichever one you choose. But only one. The spell cannot be redone, so… this is your chance."

"That means…"

"That we can be together again, my love." She smiled at him.

"This is how you were going to come back to me?" He took her face in his hands.

"I hadn't expected it to take this long." She looked up at him apologetically. "I had hoped it would be before there were any others, but I knew you would find a way. Now you can bring me back, so we can be together."

"But Lucy…"

"Lucy is a shadow of the woman you love. I know she was something to look at, and I don't fault you for pretending she was me sometimes, but now you can have the real thing. We can be together forever, Gabriel, isn't that what you've always wanted?" She looked up at him expectantly.

"Yes," he agreed. "For centuries, all I have wanted was to be with you." He tucked the loose hairs behind her ear so he could look into her eyes. "I never wanted any of the others, not even the one who loved me. She had your face, but she wasn't you," he said, as if not using Rosalind's name would make it less of a betrayal, or make him feel less guilty for the pain he caused her.

"I'm right here, Gabriel, we can be together, forever, live the life we always dreamed of."

"I promised Lucy… I need to save her," he argued.

"And I promised you I would be back. You promised me you would love me forever." She was getting upset, which wasn't like her.

"And I will, Belle, I will love you with my very last breath, but I lost you. You died in front of my eyes, and I have spent centuries trying to get over it, but Lucy doesn't deserve to die. She is kind and sweet and thoughtful and so much stronger than she realizes. She hasn't lived the life you got to live, finding love, and having a beautiful daughter. She was taken long before her time, because I couldn't save her then, but I am going to save her now."

"You think you love her?" Annabelle sounded surprised and jealous. "You just love the fact that she looks like me. That's it.

That's all you're feeling. We can be together forever. All you have to do is let her go."

"I can't," Gabriel argued. "I love her, but it is not because she looks like you, it is in spite of it. It breaks my heart to look into her eyes and see yours, but I love Lucy. And although I will always love Annabelle, you can't be her, because she would never even consider letting me save her over a young girl who has her entire life ahead of her... one of her descendants."

"If you loved Annabelle, it wouldn't have even been a dilemma. You would have chosen her without a second thought," Annabelle said, but she no longer looked like the woman he had spent his entire life loving. Her features distorted and her anger turned her into a vile version of the woman she pretended to be.

As the Annabelle imposter steamed and grew red, Gabriel said, "I choose to save Lucy." Knowing not only that it was the right decision, but that he never would have been able to live with himself without her. Annabelle, the real one, would have agreed.

THE WHITE ROOM DISAPPEARED, and Gabriel found himself back outside the house, with Embry calling after him.

"What is it?" he asked, rushing over.

"She's alive," Embry shared.

The wounds were gone, though her clothes were still bloody. Sam's fingers were at her throat, finding her pulse as they both watched her chest go up and down. Gabriel heard her heart beating and thought it was the loveliest sound he'd ever heard. He looked up to thank God, or whatever deity would take credit for it, but all he saw was Annabelle. The real one this time. He was sure of it, because she smiled sadly, as if she was proud of him. Realizing it wasn't really her and choosing Lucy must have been how he passed the test. Annabelle blew him one last kiss, smiled at him, and then she was gone.

CHAPTER TWENTY-EIGHT

I woke up confused and disoriented, with Sam and Embry staring at me while Gabriel looked up to the sky. It was quiet, even for a night in the country. All I could hear were crickets and grasshoppers. They seemed so far away, but also clearer than they ever sounded before.

"What happened?" I asked, trying to sit up, only to be stopped by Embry, who put his hands on my shoulders and gently put me back down.

"Maybe rest a bit more. Gabriel just brought you back from the dead," he shared, unable to control his smile.

"It worked?" I asked, looking from one to the other as it all came back to me.

"You're breathing, aren't you?" Sam smiled.

"How did you do it? I can't believe… it's gone." I brought my hands to the spot where the knife had gone in.

"How are you feeling?" Gabriel asked, joining our conversation.

"Maybe a little lightheaded, but we haven't eaten in a while," I reminded them. Embry rolled his eyes at my attempt to make light of my dying and being brought back to life, but he didn't argue with my explanation.

"We'll have a feast when you get up, any place you want." Sam looked so relieved to have me back. Gabriel did too, only I got the feeling he paid a terrible price for it.

"I'm good with getting out of here," I assured them. "Where's everyone else?"

"They crushed us, which is how he got to you," Embry explained.

"Let's get them out of here."

THE GUYS TOLD me to wait in Henry's office while they got everyone into the vehicles we came in, but I didn't like that plan. As soon as they left me alone, I put the remnants from the spell back into my bag and headed outside to join them, only slightly exploring the house on my way. Part of me wanted to look around and hopefully find out more about Annabelle and my ancestors, but the bigger part of me wanted to get as far away as possible from anything even remotely linked to Henry.

By the time I made it to the front yard, Caleb was carrying Peter to a car while Rosenberg did the same to Collin. I wondered how many times they'd both died for it to take so little time for them to come back. It was perfect though, since they were the only ones who could lift another grown adult as if they were a child.

I saw Etta leaning over Delia, who was lying on the ground with a large gash in her stomach, struggling to breathe. She put her hands over the wound and closed her eyes in concentration. A tiny light floated between the two of them before Delia took a deep breath, and I knew her wound was gone.

"That was amazing," I said, walking over.

"My job is to hide and watch as everyone I love dies, over and over again, so I can try to save them before the end comes," Etta shared, looking out at the field of her friends. Mallory looked like she might hold on a few moments longer, but everyone else was dead.

"I've got Delia," I assured Etta, allowing her to go help Mallory.

She gave me a grateful smile and said, "I'm glad you made it," before running off.

"Did we win?" Delia asked me.

"We did," I agreed, letting out my breath as I realized it was over.

Delia and I helped where we could, carrying people like Ingrid into the cars, until everyone was finally ready to go.

"WHAT WAS IT?" I cornered Gabriel while we walked back to the car. I didn't know where we were going yet, but nobody wanted to stay there a moment longer than we had to.

"What was what?" he asked, but he was still looking like he had lost something huge, as if a piece of his heart was gone forever.

"What did you have to give up so I can be here?" I took his hand so he would stop and look at me, staring right into my eyes.

"Annabelle," he admitted after a moment's hesitation.

That was not what I had been expecting.

"She isn't coming back. The spell could only be used once, and I saved you instead of saving her," he explained.

"I'm so sorry," I apologized. "I know how much you love her."

"I love you," he said.

"Yes, I'm the annoying kid you have to keep from dying, but Annabelle has been the love of your life for centuries," I said without mentioning that I had ever been anything more, however briefly.

"You're my heart," Gabriel argued. He looked down at my lips, then deep into my eyes, in that terrifying way where I feel like he can see into my soul, but he wasn't looking for anything other than permission. I nodded, subtly, but he seemed to be equally aware of me as he took a step closer and brought his hand to the side of my head, so his fingers were in my hair and his thumb rested on my cheek. He moved close, and I wanted to pinch myself, to make sure I wasn't dreaming, but then I felt his lips on mine and knew that I wasn't. "I'm never letting you go again," he promised.

"Your eyes," I realized. "They're brown," I said with a smile, getting him to smile as well before he leaned in and kissed me again.

"YOU'RE NOT RIDING WITH US?" I asked Embry when he stopped in front of the cars.

"Not this time," he agreed, a weird look on his face. It was like how Sam looked at me before the guys took me to the plantation at the beginning of the summer.

"I'll see you at the manor?" I tried, a sinking feeling growing in the pit of my stomach.

"Luce." He gave me a sad smile and my heart broke.

"You're not coming back with us, are you?"

"I love you to the moon and back, but you have grown into a magnificent young woman, and you don't need me to keep you safe anymore."

"I'll always need you," I argued, remembering how Alaric said you could choose whether you wanted to move on or die once you accomplished what you set out to do.

"You'll always *want* me," Embry corrected. "And I would stay a few years for you to get settled, but then I would stay for Clara, and you would have kids and..."

"You would just grow old watching me have the life I'm keeping you from getting back to," I let him know I understood, even if I hated it. "Is she here?" I looked around as if I could see her. I couldn't stomach the idea of him killing himself to join her, but if she was here, I wouldn't stop him from walking into the light with her.

"She's been waiting a long time," he agreed.

"Thank her for me." I bridged the distance between us and let him take me in his arms one last time.

"I am so proud of you, Lucy. You really are incredible."

"I was raised by a collective of really awesome people." I smiled through tears.

"It shows," he teased, squeezing me tight before going over to Gabriel, who was checking the vehicles to make sure we had everyone. I couldn't hear what they said, but Gabriel gave him a sad smile before they hugged.

Embry walked off towards the gazebo, lifted his arm like he was reaching for someone's outstretched hand, and then he was gone.

EPILOGUE

TEN AND A HALF YEARS LATER...

It felt weird being back at my high school, especially since everything looked the same as it had back when I knew nothing about magic or the world of Gifted. Everything except the students. The freshmen today looked like college students had when I was in school. Or maybe I just felt that way because Clara was the one graduating, and no matter how many milestones I watched her reach, I still thought of her as my baby sister.

"There they are." Gabriel waved over to where Sam and Deanna were saving us seats, his fiery red hair and her platinum pixie making them hard to miss. Gabriel put his hand out to help me up the bleachers, which made me roll my eyes, even if I have been a little clumsier lately. He says I glow, but I'm pretty sure I look like a whale and he's just too in love with me to mention it.

"How was Italy?" Deanna asked of our babymoon, once the hugs were out of the way.

"I think I ate my weight in pasta, but it was so worth it," I shared before tickling Ethan, who was in his father's lap. I don't know what promise or mission had made Sam Gifted, but not long after we got back from Henry's, we noticed him growing older right along with Deanna, as if I hadn't watched him die. I

201

know from Gabriel that you don't lose your Gift when you become human again, but Sam never mentioned his.

"It shows," Sam teased, nodding to my very pregnant stomach, which garnered a fit of giggles.

ONCE CLARA'S graduation was over, we went back to the manor for a celebratory dinner, but my sister-niece spent most of the meal going over everything she should do on her graduation trip to Europe. She and her friends were trying to cover twelve countries in twenty-one days, and I happen to have been to all of them. During my summer breaks from Harvard, Gabriel and I chose a different place I'd always dreamed of visiting and explored it to our heart's content. He almost always knew someone in the area who could show us how the locals live, but most of the time we just wandered around and stumbled onto amazing little gems off the beaten path. Now that I wasn't going to die from a Curse and Gabriel wasn't going to live forever, we made it a point to live our lives to the fullest.

"And which one was your favorite?" Clara asked me with her best friend, Eloise, hanging on every word. "Italy?" she guessed, since the babymoon was our second trip to Embry's birthplace.

"It's very romantic," I agreed, looking over to Deanna to gauge her reaction, but she was no longer in the dining room. "It's the perfect place to escape with someone you love, but I've been told it's also a cool place to be wooed by a—"

"For she's a jolly good fellow..." the singing interrupted my suggestion that Clara have an Italian fling, which was probably for the best.

"You still haven't figured out a better song?" Clara asked as we finished our off-key rendition and Deanna put the cake down in front of her.

"Found it!" Sam rushed into the dining room with a video

camera and pointed it at his daughter. "We're going to have to do the singing over again," he told us.

"Dad," Clara said, making two syllables of the word as she rolled her eyes. It was the standard response from a teenager embarrassed by her parents when her friends come over. But unlike her friends who laughed with her, Clara and I both knew how lucky she was to have her dad there to fuss over her.

"One day, you'll be happy you can look back at how cute you were as a child. All the fun, happy memories," I pointed out as Gabriel came and wrapped his arms around me from behind, resting his hands on my stomach, and his head on my shoulder.

"They hardly ever use them to embarrass you," Gabriel added, teasing her to get a smile. I watched her friends from school stare at him with googly eyes until he caught them, at which point they looked away and giggled.

"Did your dad follow you around with a video camera?" Clara asked me.

"My dad wasn't as cool as yours." She knew my dad wasn't in the picture now, but she assumed he used to be, like Sam's dad. She rolled her eyes at me, disagreeing with my assessment of her father.

"Also, we were born in a time when video cameras were these huge things you had to lug around, then transfer the tapes onto VHS if you wanted to watch them," Deanna shared, with Ethan now perched on her hip. He was trying so hard not to fall asleep because of all the excitement, but it might be a little too much for a four-year-old.

"Can we watch them?" Clara asked, always curious about the past, probably because we never talked about it. Especially not with her.

"Not unless you have a VCR," Gabriel said apologetically, knowing full well that we had one back at the plantation. I went through all the old home videos and photographs when Gabriel and I moved into our newly renovated home. I wouldn't say we had a shrine to the women that came before me, but we had a room that housed all my ancestor's artefacts. One day, I would tell our kids about them, the women who made me who I am, and ultimately brought Gabriel and I together.

"What's a VCR?" Clara asked with a smile.

"Way before your time," I assured her, knowing that she knew and was just trying to make us feel our age.

"You guys must be really old."

"You have no idea, sweetie," Gabriel said, kissing her forehead. He sometimes slipped, and Clara would look at him funny, as if she was about to point out there was no way he met JFK, but then she would decide against it and let him backtrack to say he read it in a book or saw it in a movie. She probably knew way more than any of us gave her credit for, but she was smart, and seemed to understand that it wasn't a pleasant story we were keeping from her.

After Sam got his video of Clara blowing out her candles and making a wish, he turned the camera on me. I was about to wish Clara a happy birthday on camera, assuming it was a video testimonial, but they started singing again.

"My birthday isn't for months," I argued as they put a large cake in front of me.

"It's not a birthday cake." Clara eyed my stomach as I read the icing.

"A baby shower?" I turned to Deanna.

"Clara didn't want us to do it while she was in Europe, and today was the only day everyone could show up."

"I love you kid." I took Clara in for a hug. "But this is your graduation."

"And you can tell that to my niece or nephew, so they know I love them the most." She gave me a big smile before nodding over to where Keisha, Ingrid, Etta, Delia, Angela, Jen, and Sarah were standing with their husbands, and some of my co-workers from the hospital. I was touched, even before Gabriel brought

Charlie over, followed by Eric, his wife, and their two adorable sons.

I got up from the table and went to hug them all. It was getting harder and harder with Keisha; her twins with Tennison were due any day now.

AFTER THE CAKE, Clara went to celebrate with her friends from school, while Deanna hosted an alcohol- and guy-friendly baby shower. It was very entertaining watching my husband try to figure out modern-day diapers, since the last time he changed one was probably centuries ago.

I ended up by the doorway into the living room, watching all my worlds intermingling. Delia and her husband were laughing with Keisha and Tennison, Caleb and Etta were in their glory playing hide and seek with Ethan, Ingrid was using her Gift of illusions on Sarah, who was staring at a painting like it was a television screen... even Alaric was promising Deanna that Clara could come to him if anything happened while she was in London.

I loved seeing the house so full of people, but it was always at the big occasions like these that I got nostalgic, remembering the people we lost, and how far we've come.

It took me a long time to stop blaming myself for some of the things I did, but instead of dwelling on it, I now try to make up for it, by putting more good out into the world than I took away. It means a lot of late nights at the hospital, but it isn't so bad when your husband is there with you. And Clara makes sure we take Sundays off to be there for a family dinner.

We missed a few last year, when Gabriel and I spent six months in Africa. Alaric's charity sponsored a mission to build houses and provide medical aid, so Gabriel and I went as doctors, Caleb brought his muscles, and I have a suspicion Etta came in case I needed emergency healing. Luckily, Kiara's Curse was indeed lifted, and I made it to the ridiculous party everyone threw for my twenty-ninth birthday. Many people asked why we were going all out for a random, non-milestone birthday, but most of them understood.

"Where are you?" Gabriel asked me when he came over with a sizeable piece of cake and two forks, waking me from my daydream.

"I'm back," I said with a smile, grabbing the fork to take a bite.

"Want me to whisk you away from all the celebrating?" He offered before swallowing an abnormally large piece.

"I like it," I assured him. "A wise old man once told me to celebrate everything."

"Embry was right." He smiled sadly at me. "But I'm not sure he would appreciate you calling him an old man."

"There's absolutely nothing wrong with getting old. I happen to be married to a much older gentleman who is waiting for me to catch up."

"Is that so?" he asked, putting the plate down to take me in his arms.

"I have my whole life ahead of me, and I plan on taking advantage of that with you," I said, leaning in for a kiss. When we pulled apart, I looked into his eyes, his beautiful brown eyes, and brushed my fingers through his slightly graying sideburns.

"If you keep obsessing over my gray hairs, you'll give me a complex," he warned.

"You know I love watching you go gray. It reminds me that…"

"That we're all going to die?" he finished for me.

"No, that we get to live. We aren't surviving anymore, we're settling down, having kids and families, then one day, in a very long time, we will die peacefully in our sleep of old age."

"Sounds perfect," he said before kissing me.

The End

***

Turn the page for the
Bearers of the Crescent Moon Family Tree
***

Lucy's curse may be broken, but she — and many others from the
Owens Chronicles — return in
The Gifted Chronicles

Alison Carmichael has her future lined up, from taking care of her sister to the job waiting for her at her dad's firm once she graduates. But when she discovers she has a supernatural Gift – of reliving memories by touching objects – it puts everything she thought she knew into question. Including her budding romance with Tristan Davis, a mysterious, yet very swoonworthy out of towner.

Instead of going to California with her family, Alison takes a summer internship solving cold cases at her local precinct, where Dr. Graciela Goncalves promises to teach her to control her Gift. As Alison learns more about this new world and her place within it, she finds herself working on more current cases and biting off more than she can chew.

When those closest to her turn up as victims, can Alison put the pieces together and solve the puzzle before it's too late?

Find out in this 'magical adventure that intertwines romance and mystery'!

Get First Life now!

Owens Family Tree

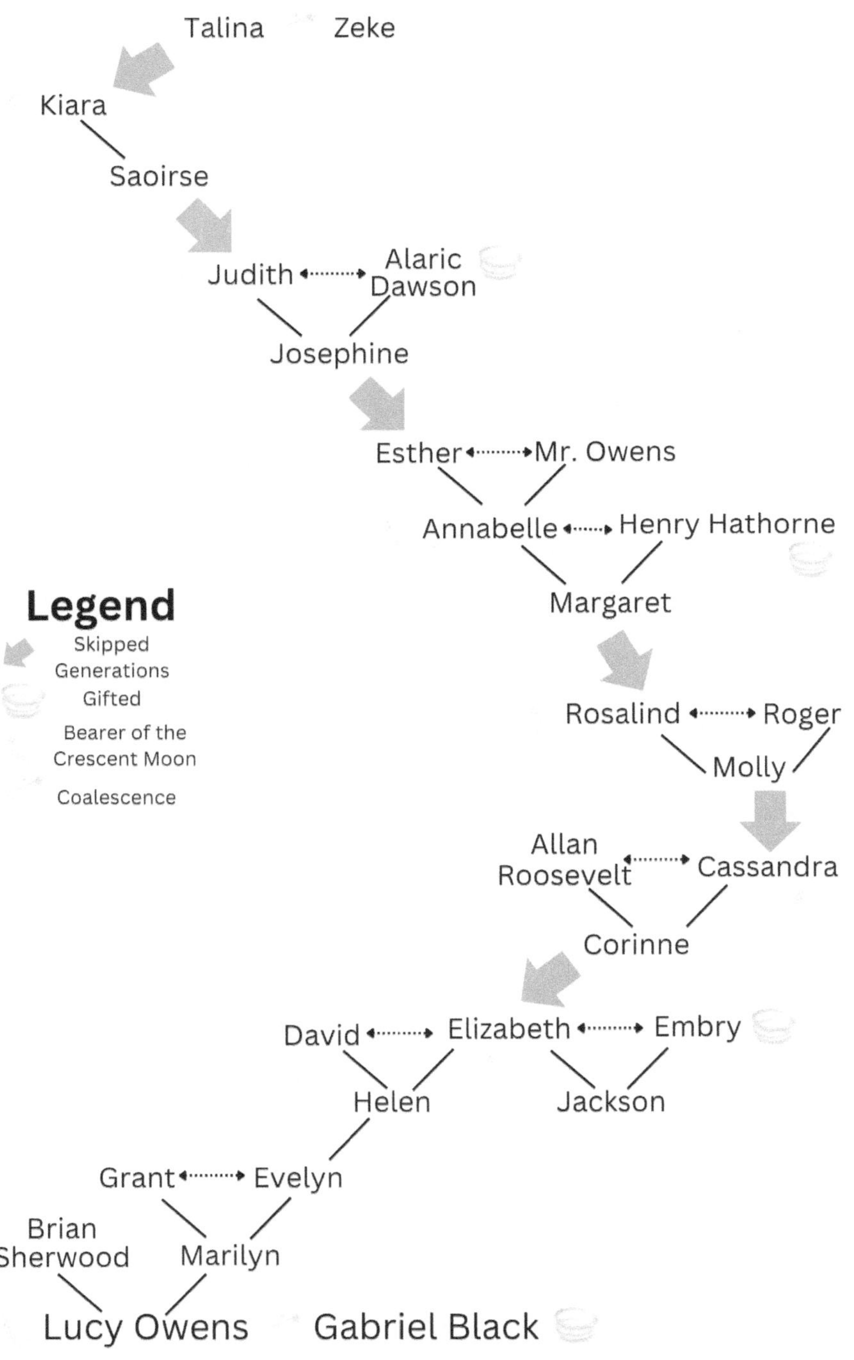

Legend

AUTHOR'S NOTE

Thank you so much for reading the final volume of The Owens Chronicles. I came up with the idea of the Gifted over a decade ago, when I wanted supernatural beings who lived for centuries, but weren't vampires. I loved coming up with historical figures who could have been Gifted, as well as all of the intricacies a system like this could present.

I can't believe how much the story has evolved, and how many stories in their universe I have left to tell. Delia is one of my favourite characters, yet you still know nothing about her…maybe someday. For now, I hope you enjoyed The Owens Chronicles. I hope the books let you escape and get lost in another world for a bit. And I hope you find your own happy ending. Or better yet, I hope you make it ;)

If you enjoyed Legacy, it would mean the world to me if you could tell your friends about it. Maybe leave a review on the platform you got it from, Goodreads, or Bookbub. Indie books live and die by word of mouth & reviews, and I hope Lucy's story gets to live.

Thank you again for letting my stories into your life. It was a pleasure sharing them with you. Happy reading!

ACKNOWLEDGMENTS

My acknowledgements feel redundant, but I am really lucky to have an incredible group of people who show up for me time and time again.

My eternal gratitude goes to my mom, who rereads the books as often as I do, and offers me her undying love and support. I would be nothing without you.

Rikki, it means so much to me that you not only take the time to read my books with everything else you have going on, but that you BETA read them as well. You give me such useful feedback, and the fact that you like the books means more to me than you'll ever know. As far as I am concerned, you are a superwoman, for a million different reasons.

Adeline, I have never met you, but I so appreciate you BETA reading the book. Your kind words and enthusiasm have given me so much joy and confidence. Thank you!

Though not involved in the production of this book, I still need to thank some very important people:

Moe, who has every book I ever write on preorder. Louise, who responds to every newsletter.

Linda, who buys the book in multiple formats so she can read one and leave the others at hotels for people to discover.

I also want to thank Steve, Paul, Rikki, my mom, my dad, Linda, Jean-Guy, Liz, J-F, Arsen, Gohar, Sam, Melanie, Luigi, Laurie, Teresa, Pierrette, Shiva, Sacha, Alanna, Rosina, Donna, Kimberlie, Desiree, Jamie, Louise, Warren, Nelson, Christie, and everyone else who shared my posts and talked about the books on social media.

And the biggest thank you, from the absolute bottom of my heart and every fibre of my being to each and every single one of you who bought a copy and read my book. I definitely did not expect the outpouring of support that I have received and it sure makes this girl feel all warm and fuzzy inside.

Thank you <3

9 781989 950029